THE HIGHLANDER'S *Hope*

A CONTEMPORARY HIGHLAND ROMANCE
BOOK ONE

CALI MACKAY

The Highlander's Hope
by Cali MacKay|
Copyright © 2012 by Cali MacKay
Published by Cali MacKay
http://calimackay.com

Printed in the United States of America
First Printing, 2012, edition 1.2
ISBN: 978-1-940041-08-7

Contents

I wanted to thank my sweet, understanding and horribly sarcastic husband for all his support, my two lovely girls for being so good when I'm trying to write, and my fellow writers for supporting me and combing over my stories.

For more information or to join a mailing list for updates, please visit http://calimackay.com.

CHAPTER
One

UST DANCED UPON the shards of light that pierced the ancient hall of the library archives. As if calling out to her, the words on the page taunted and teased, daring Catriona to find the secret they had long held safe. One would think it a simple letter between lovers torn apart at a time of war. However, Cat saw the clues woven through the endearments. She was one step closer to solving a centuries-old mystery and finding a priceless treasure.

The pounding of her heart competed with the flutters in her stomach. It could be a historic find of epic proportions, and yet it was so much more than that to her, having been raised on her grandmother's stories of highland heroes and ancient lands.

The Highlander's Hope. A necklace crusted with emeralds, diamonds and sapphires, it had once been destined to fund the Scottish rising against the English. But that was before the battle of Culloden shattered

Scotland's dreams of retaking the English throne, and the necklace was lost.

Cat was now one step closer. All she had to do was piece the puzzle together and find the Hope.

"Crap!" Cat maneuvered her car to the edge of the narrow road, with the growing suspicion that the flopping sound killing the rhythm of her music meant she had a flat tire.

Being late for her appointment with Callum MacCraigh could ruin everything, and she was still hours away from the highland town of Dunmuir. Everything hinged on getting access to the MacCraigh estate and family records, and without the clan's cooperation, she'd never find the jewels.

Having left at the crack of dawn, she'd already been on the road most of the day, the drive from Cambridge to the north of Scotland long enough for her butt to have gone numb hours ago.

Muttering curses under her breath, she pulled her hoodie up over her head and stepped out into the pouring rain. Luckily she had a spare, even if she'd never had the occasion to change one. Couldn't be that difficult to get the blasted thing on.

She hauled the tiny spare out from the back of her car, relieved to see that, at the very least, it was inflated, and then grabbed the metal doohickey for undoing the nuts. With the opening fitted over one of the bolts holding her flat hostage, she grabbed the metal arm and yanked with all her might. A muscle in her back twitched in protest as she strained in effort, but to no avail. Was it rusted or had years of gunk and grime cemented it in place?

"Righty-tighty, lefty- loosey."

She tried again, with a grunt of frustration, water dripping off her nose with an evil tickle, as the bolt finally gave way. Relieved, she loosened it and stuck it in her pocket. One down, three to go. The next two came off with relative ease, if she ignored the scraped knuckles and broken nail. The last one, however, refused to budge.

Bent over and once more straining against the iron, she didn't notice the car whizzing around the corner, coming right at her, until it was nearly on top of her. She jumped out of the way, landing in a puddle of mud as the silver Jag screeched to a halt.

Cursing, she tried to slow her tripping heart and pulled herself to her feet, wiping her face in a futile attempt to rid herself of the nasty puddle water, even though she did little more than smear the mud.

Now out of his car, the other driver was stalking towards her. "Are ye hurt?"

She took a quick account of all her body parts. "No, I'm fine, other than being covered in muck and mud."

Any concern he'd shown blazed up in his fury. "What the bloody hell were ye doing in the middle of the road? Have ye lost yer mind, woman?"

"Me? Are you kidding? There is *no* way this is my fault, and I was *not* in the middle of the road." With her own temper rearing up to match his, she barely took in the handsome face and blue eyes. "You could have killed me, coming around the corner that fast."

"And ye'd not have been in danger if ye'd been sensible and parked farther down the road, rather than in the blind spot by the wall."

Dark tousled hair. Touch of stubble on a strong jaw. Tall. Well-muscled. Sexy. Why did he look vaguely familiar?

"Well, I'll be sure to keep that in mind when choosing when and where my car will next break down." She squinted to keep a nasty drip from invading her eye. There surely had to be sheep dung in that mud. She'd never get clean, and her mind was already running down the dozens of bacteria and diseases that would likely overwhelm her body's defenses.

As if suddenly remembering his manners, he tilted his head towards her flat. "Ye need a hand then?"

Like she'd accept his help after he'd tried to blame her for the entire incident. With arms crossed in front of her chest and her head cocked to the side, she said, "I'll manage just fine, thank you for asking. And do try to not kill anyone on your way to wherever it is you're going."

"Hmph." Without another word, he stalked back to his car and took off like the furies of hell were on his tail, his tires spinning and spitting gravel onto the wet road.

By the time she got to Dunmuir and walked into the inn, she was colder than a polar bear's butt after sitting on a glacier, and filthier than a three year old making mud pies. Nearly dying had left her more than a little on edge; however, all that mattered was that she hadn't missed her appointment with Callum MacCraigh. She even had enough time to get ready and collect her thoughts.

"Here, sit by the fire and get yerself warmed up." Mrs. Gordon, a motherly type in her sixties, tried to steer her towards the chair, but Cat shook her head no.

"I'm filthy and don't want to get your sofa dirty. I'll be fine once I get cleaned up." The thought of soaking in a hot tub sent goose bumps crawling across her skin. She quickly signed the papers that were put in front of her, not wanting to delay that bath any more than she had to.

"Aye, of course. The room has an en suite, but be sure to let me know if ye need anything else. If ye set aside yer laundry, I'll be happy to have it done for you." She handed Cat the key to her room. "It'll be the second floor on the left. Follow it to the end."

"Thank you."

So far from any major city, the inn was larger than she'd imagined, and had been recently renovated with a modern feel that still gave a nod to its history and past. It was a pretty seaside town that saw its share of tourists in the summer, though most only came for daily excursions to see the standing stones not far from town.

She let herself into the room, abandoned her things by the bed, and headed straight for the bath. Her knees practically went weak at the sight of the tub. It was deep and jetted, and the water was plenty hot. Fighting with her wet clothes as the tub filled, she finally managed to pry them off, leaving them abandoned in a filthy heap on the tile floor. Not bothering to grab a book, she slipped into the hot water, her skin burning from the extremes in temperature, her body yet to thaw.

By the time she'd scrubbed herself clean and let the heat of the water soak through to her bones, she felt like herself again. Excitement bubbled within her, knowing she could soon have access to records few had seen before. She just needed to find more concrete information on where the jewels were hidden. Tansy, her research assistant, would be beside herself if she actually managed to find them. Cat knew better than to trust her colleagues with such a find, but Tansy was the one exception.

With her makeup and hair done, Cat slipped on her dark boot-legged jeans and cashmere sweater, the robin's egg blue of her top playing against her dark mahogany locks. Casual, but put together.

With the address plugged into the GPS in her car, it wasn't long before she found herself at her destination and pulling down a long gravel drive. The home could have graced any postcard or travel brochure, quintessentially Scottish with its stone walls and embattlements, harkening to a time long gone.

She climbed the granite steps of the manor to its front door, letting the heavy knocker drop against the brass plate. Her stomach fluttered with nerves as she waited, but it didn't take long for someone to answer. An older gentleman stood before her, his blue eyes keen and a giant scruffy dog at his side.

"You must be Ms.—pardon me, Dr. Ross. Callum MacCraigh, and this here is Duncan." He tilted his head towards the grey beast. "Come in, come in."

"Thank you. And please, call me Catriona—or Cat." She shook his hand with a smile, and followed behind him.

Excitement sparked as she took in the home, her thoughts running amock as she imagined hidden clues and secret treasures. Tapestries hung on the walls, as did paintings hundreds of years old. The place felt grand and well-loved, no signs of neglect despite the age.

"I can't thank you enough for agreeing to speak with me."

"The pleasure's all mine, my dear. We seldom get visitors, and certainly no one who'd be interested in hearing any of the stories I have to tell." Callum shrugged, not looking too worried that he didn't normally have an audience.

Callum led her into the great room, the ceilings high and the wooden beams exposed to add a rustic charm. However, her focus immediately went to the stone fireplace which traveled the height of the entire wall, a roaring fire nestled within. He showed her to a seat close enough to feel the heat of the flames and ward off the damp.

"It gets cold this time of year, and it can be hard to keep this big drafty place warm. I hope you won't get chilled."

"This is perfect. Thank you." When the dog nudged her leg, she gave his head a long scratch. The dog's ears then perked up and he dashed across the room, taking the corner so fast his legs skidded out from under him on the hardwood floors.

"That'll be my son, Iain. I told him you were coming, since he's studied our family's history and could be of use to yer research. He's actually the one you should be talking to and will be happy to help ye in any way he can." Callum got to his feet. "Iain, come here, lad."

She stood and turned to face him, when her smile faded and a furious heat rushed to her face. "You've got to be kidding me."

He squinted as he took her in, and then let out a scoff. "Ah! You clean up well, I'll give you that. Barely recognized ye."

"Ye've met?" His father looked at the two of them in question, confusion and humor lining his face.

"Aye, Da. But only for a moment and at the time I didn't realize I had the pleasure of speaking to the esteemed Dr. Ross." A smug smile tugged at his lips, his blue eyes alight with amusement. He reached out and took her hand. "It's a pleasure to put a name to the face, since we weren't properly introduced earlier."

"The pleasure's mine." Cat tried to erase the sarcasm from her voice, but wasn't sure she was entirely successful. She couldn't risk jeopardizing everything over a stupid incident.

And then it occurred to her why the bastard looked vaguely familiar. She'd been looking at the MacCraigh clan, but not once had she thought to associate them with *the* Iain MacCraigh—Scotland's most eligible bachelor, businessman and playboy extraordinaire. That would teach her to ignore the tabloids. Her mind never put the two together.

"I'll fetch us a cup of tea." Iain didn't bother waiting for anyone's response, but spun around and headed back out the way he came.

Callum sat back down, and she followed suit. "He'd be my oldest. There's another son, Malcolm, but he lives in Edinburgh. Comes to visit often enough. And then there's Moira. She's away in Paris, though I keep hoping she'll someday return. Can't really blame her. There's not much for the young folk around here, and I'm sure if it weren't for me and this place, Iain would've also left long ago."

"Is it just the two of you then?" She suspected it might be the case. No one else had poked their head in, and the house had a bit of an empty feel to it.

"Aye, it is. My wife passed a few years back. It's an awfully big house for just the two of us, but I'm hoping Iain will eventually settle down. It'd be nice to see new life brought into this old place." He gave her a kind smile. "Enough about me. You came here for a reason, and I doubt it was to hear me rambling 'bout nothing at all. What is it I can help you with?"

Cat couldn't tell him the real reason for her research—not yet anyway—though she could skirt the truth. Telling anyone of her plans now would only make it more difficult to keep treasure hunters and other researchers at bay. It was a lesson she'd learned the hard way, and was still furious that her ex had taken all the credit for a past research project when she had done most of the work. She wouldn't make the same mistake twice, especially not with a find as important as the Highlander's Hope.

"My research has led me to believe that your clan may have played more of a role during the Jacobite uprising than most know. I'd like to find definitive proof, but would need access to your clan's documents and estate."

The old man's eye's brightened with enthusiasm. "Now that's exciting news, lass. Whatever it is ye need, ye can have full access to it. And like I said, Iain will be happy to help ye any way he can."

Cat somehow doubted that.

As if the mere mention of his name was enough to summon the devil, Iain walked in with a tray of tea and set it down on the table between them, sitting by his father's side with Duncan at their feet.

Callum turned to his son to give him the good news. "Dr. Ross thinks she's found evidence of our clan playing a more important role during Culloden than originally believed."

He looked at her with no love or enthusiasm. "Is that so?"

"It is." She tried not to be curt with him, but the man seemed to bring out the worst in her. How they'd manage to work together was beyond her. "I'm looking into the history of the Jacobites and, in particular, how funding was raised amongst the clans prior to the arrival of Prince Charles Edward Stewart."

"I don't know why ye'd think our clan any different to the others. The majority of the clans this far into the highlands supported the uprising any way they could, despite the little most had to live on." His eyes narrowed in suspicion. "Given all yer fancy degrees, I'd think ye'd already know that."

"Well, yes, my doctorate on Scottish history did require me to actually learn a little about Scottish history—but I assure you the circumstances are a little different when it comes to your clan. I wouldn't be here otherwise." It was impossible to keep the annoyance from her voice.

"Don't mind him, lass. He's always had a sharp tongue in that head of his and not enough common sense or manners." Callum gave his son a sideways glance that spoke volumes.

"My apologies. I meant no offense." Except that his tone told her he didn't mean a word he'd just spoken. Iain poured the tea, even though his wary gaze was on her rather than on the cups before him. "So do ye have any proof of this importance and why our clan's so different?"

She couldn't risk telling him the true reason, and yet she had no doubt he'd see through any lies. Iain seemed far too intelligent and distrustful a man, and she was sure he'd miss nothing. Best to skirt the truth then, and see if it would be enough to gain her the access she needed.

"I've found some information regarding the movement of funds leading up to the revolution and think your clan may have played a significant role in the transfer. It's that role that I want to investigate—and the route of the monies. It could be of considerable historic importance and your clan would have been key."

Iain sat back in his chair, his legs stretched out before him as he sipped his tea. "Ye'll pardon my saying so, but I'm not buying it, lass. The war was centuries ago, and I'd imagine historians have looked at every aspect of the war, a dozen times over. So if ye have new information, I'd like to know what it is."

She couldn't tell him. There was still too little to go on. Not enough clues. "Honestly, I would love to tell you, but first I need to know that I'm on the right track."

Iain let out a scoff and shook his head, but she pressed on, hoping to convince him. "Truth be told, I can't do this without your help. Everything leads to your clan—to this home and this land. I can't take the next step without more information. But I swear, once I'm a bit more certain of what I've found, I'll tell you everything I know."

It was as honest as she could be for now. She just hoped it would be enough.

"Son, I probably should've asked ye first, but I've already promised the lass our help, and truth is I want to help her. I'd like to know what role our clan played in the uprising."

Iain reached out and put a hand on his father's arm with a sigh, his words still holding onto a hint of his annoyance. "Very well then, if it'll make you happy."

CHAPTER Two

I AIN WONDERED WHAT Cat was truly up to. Clearly, she was being less than honest with them, and yet his father seemed smitten, even inviting her to dine with them for the evening.

At any other time, he wouldn't have minded helping her, but his brother had gotten himself into a world of trouble and the last thing he needed was a snooping historian. If the tabloids found out the trouble his family was in, they'd have a field day. Though his reputation as a shrewd businessman was never harmed by the string of models he dated, his brother's troubles could have a real impact on his business dealings.

Looking across the table at his father and Cat chatting like old friends made him want to curse. He couldn't deny the old man the pleasure, for there was little to make him happy as of late. It just meant he'd have to keep a sharp eye on her, and try to make the most of it—for his father's sake.

With dinner over, he got to his feet to clear the table.

"Here, let me give you a hand." Cat gathered the dirty dishes from their meal and followed him to the kitchen, but not before throwing a smile in his father's direction.

Curses.

"I appreciate the help." Iain put the dishes in the sink, and then took the ones she was carrying. "Listen, about earlier today—on the road. I'm sorry, aye? I'd have been happy to change your flat."

She shrugged, tucking a dark curl behind her ear, avoiding his gaze. "I didn't really give you the chance."

"I nearly killed ye. It left me shaken." By the gods, he'd played it in his head over and over in an endless loop since it happened. Despite not wanting her around, nearly hitting her had left him mortified. "I hope ye'll be more careful next time. You can't go parking around blind turns like that."

She may have avoided looking at him earlier, but he now had her full attention, her green eyes locked on his, fire raging within them.

"Really? You want to have *that* conversation again?" Her cheeks flushed as she cocked her head to the side in question. "I can't believe you're still trying to pin this whole thing on me. Maybe if you weren't driving like a maniac, you'd have seen me."

He took a deep breath to keep from yelling and did his best to ignore the throbbing vein at his temple. "I've driven down that road a million times and could do it blind—but only if there's no one in the middle of the road. Anyone with a wee bit of common sense would know you don't park around a turn where ye'll not be seen. Even with a flat, you certainly could have driven it another ten feet down the road."

"So now I have no common sense and it was all my fault? You really are an arrogant jerk." With hands on curvy hips and her eyes ablaze, she looked ready to unleash her wrath.

So why was it his lips could do nothing but quirk into a smile?

"What are you grinning at? Do you think this is funny? It took me hours to soak the cold and mud from my skin."

The girl was furious with him, and yet he could not help himself. Something about her made him want to push her buttons—all of them. "I wouldn't think ye'd have a hard time heating up with that temper. Yer cheeks have gone so red, yer freckles have gone into hiding."

She swore under her breath and then spun on her heels, stalking out of the room. With a quick jaunt, he caught up to her, gently grabbing her arm to stop her, not quite ready to have his fun come to an end. "It'd be a pity to go before you find what ye're looking for. But please, don't let me stop ye. I'm sure ye have other ways of finding what ye're after."

"I may need your help for my research, but if you think I'm going to beg and plead, or kiss your *wee Scottish arse*, then you're going to be waiting a long time."

A laugh escaped him, despite it all. "I'm sorry. I was just teasing ye. It's absolutely true—I'm a total arse."

He saw the internal debate going on inside that pretty head of hers. She was still furious with him, and yet there was her research to consider. Or was there more to it? She was putting up with an awful lot.

His gut told him she was up to something, but what? Maybe it'd be best to string her along until he could get more information. So he tried again to get her to stay and to avoid the tongue lashing he'd get from his father for upsetting a guest, no matter that he was a grown man.

"I really am sorry. I take full responsibility for the incident. I was in a hurry, and being familiar with the road, I wasn't paying as much attention as I should've been. Truce?"

She let out a weary sigh. "Truce."

CALI MACKAY

Iain stared at his laptop screen, cursing his brother for making such a mess of things. His email back to Malcolm was harsh, but he'd not mince words when the fool had just put their entire estate in jeopardy. Things were a mess, and it was Malcolm's fault—and his father's for being gullible enough to believe whatever lies Malcolm fed him. Neither their father nor sister knew that things now verged on the brink of disaster. He'd try to spare them as long as possible, and with luck, he'd manage to turn things around before anyone found out.

Cat. It was as if the gods had decided to play a cruel joke on him. She could be trouble—in more ways than one. And though she could prove a pleasant enough distraction from his troubles, she brought out the worst in him. The only other woman he'd ever antagonized like that was his sister when they were still children. Yet tonight, he'd barely been able to resist such games, even though he knew better than to let his guard down.

He knew there was more to her visit than she was telling him, and with the mess his brother was in, he couldn't afford to have it leak to the media. His business rivals would pounce, and his clients would second guess his abilities—as if it wasn't bad enough that he now had to find the funds to bail his brother out of his troubles. It didn't sound like the men Malcolm had involved himself with were the patient and under-standing sort.

As for Cat's research... he gave it some thought. His clan had always been small in number, even before Culloden further diminished their numbers. Yet despite their clan size, they'd yielded a fair amount of influence in the highlands, and Iain had studied their history enough to suspect what Cat might be after. She'd mentioned the funds destined for the revolution, and that was enough to tell him she was looking for the jewels.

Well, best of luck to her. There was no reason to think his family was connected to the jewels, and others had certainly gone looking amongst the highland clans, only to come up empty-handed.

Finding any information on the necklace would be a long shot, but if she did find it, it might turn out to be the lifeline he needed. If found on their lands, the jewels would belong to his clan, even if it was her find.

A knock at his office door had him looking up. "Da. Are you off to bed then?"

"Aye, in just a bit." He came in and sat down. "Will you be meeting with the lass again?"

Iain spun his chair around to face his father. "She's going to come by in the morning to review any information we have from before and after the time of Culloden."

His father pinned him with a stern look. "I hope ye'll be nicer to her this time around. If I hear ye've gone and chased her off, I won't be happy, Iain. Yer Ma wouldn't have tolerated you disrespecting any guest of this house, and I won't put up with it either. Ye hear?"

"Don't go worrying yerself, Da. I promise I'll try to be on my best behavior and not antagonize her." Iain gave his father a reassuring smile.

Callum had clearly enjoyed Cat's company. Too often it was just the two of them knocking about the empty house, and Iain was usually busy with work to be of any real company. Luckily, he could get most of his business conducted from home, even if he did have to travel from time to time.

Not yet done, Callum pulled him from his thoughts for another scolding. "I hadn't realized ye'd already met—and by all accounts you weren't much nicer to her then, either."

Iain had to laugh, recalling the state of her covered in mud and dripping wet. "Now that wasn't entirely my fault, though ye're right. I could have been nicer."

Giving her a bit more thought, Iain continued. "When she spoke to ye… did she say what she was looking for?"

"Nae. Nothing more than what she said tonight. Why? What are ye thinking, lad?"

Iain shrugged. "Nothing. I was just curious is all."

Callum got to his feet. "Just make sure ye keep yer curiosity honorable, aye? I may be old, and ye may have been rude, but I'm not blind. There's heat between the two of ye, so be sure to behave yerself."

"She's pretty, but definitely not my type. Far too uptight and... scholarly." Iain waved away his father's concerns, thinking of the proper sweater, her hair tamed up and out of the way with some fancy twist when it was desperate to escape and go wild. All she needed was a pair of glasses and a string of pearls, and she could pass for a librarian.

His father scowled at him, his eyes narrowed in annoyance. "Aye, ye wouldn't want someone smart and pretty. Ye've clearly chosen far more wisely in the past."

Iain shook his head with a smile. "Good night to ye, Da."

With thoughts of highland treasure and pretty librarians bouncing around his head, Iain headed off to the library with Duncan lazily trailing behind him. With two levels of books, a catwalk for ease of use, a comfortable sofa and a large stone fireplace, this room was easily Iain's favorite.

Duncan sat in front of the fireplace, and looked at him in question.

"No, Duncan. I'm not building a fire this late at night."

Duncan responded with a noise that sounded like a cross between a yawn and yelp, followed by a cock of his head as his sad brown eyes attempted to guilt Iain into doing his bidding.

Iain ignored him and wandered to the shelf where they kept the oldest books.

Duncan barked, and then barked again, the noise deafening when backed by the lungs tucked in that massive chest.

"Seriously, dog?"

He got a rapid thwapping of tail in response. Fully aware the pup would keep bugging him until a fire was lit, Iain quickly got one going with the knowledge he too would enjoy it. The nights were cold this far north, even if it was only October.

With the dog content, Iain wandered back to the bookshelf housing dozens of books dating back ages and generations. It had been years since he last went through them, and though they were in decent shape, he tried not to handle them too often. When he'd gone through them in the past it wasn't with an eye for finding anything in particular. Now, however, he'd take another look, keeping a keen eye out for any clues that might give up their mystery.

It would likely lead nowhere, but Cat had his curiosity going, and if he was stuck with her snooping around, then he might as well make the most of it. The stories he'd heard regarding the bejeweled necklace had never mentioned his family. So why did she think his clan had been somehow involved? He supposed it could be true—or was she looking for something else.

His ancestors had been loyal Jacobites. Then again, nearly every highland clan had supported the cause of Bonnie Prince Charlie and had wanted him to take back the throne. She had found something—but what? And could the information be trusted? Could *she* be trusted?

Time would tell.

CHAPTER Three

ESPITE THE IMPENDING excitement of looking for the jewels, Cat would still need a cup of coffee to wake her up. The anticipation of what she'd find had kept her up most of the night, and she'd only managed to drift off to sleep mere hours before her wakeup call. Her head was in a fog, and if she didn't get some caffeine quickly, she'd fall asleep on the way to her appointment with Iain.

Iain. She cursed the smile that tugged at her lips, and reminded herself just how infuriating the man had been. Absolutely, without a doubt, the most frustrating man she'd met in a very long time. At least he was willing to help her. That was huge—and for that, she wouldn't write him off as a complete jerk.

Needing that cup of coffee and some breakfast, Cat quickly showered and got dressed, twisting her hair up and out of the way with a pretty clip, before wandering downstairs.

"Morning. If ye're looking for yer friend, he's having a bite to eat in the dining room." Mrs. Gordon gave her a smile while tidying the papers behind the counter. "It's a buffet, so help yerself. And if ye need anything, just let me know."

Cat was confused. She thought she was meeting with Iain at his home. "Iain's here?"

"Iain? Iain MacCraigh? Och, no. He was an Englishman." She shook her head and tapped at the computer. "Says here his name is Dr. James Tanner."

Cat's face flushed with anger, as she wondered if he'd followed her up from Cambridge. There was no way in hell she'd let him swoop in and find the jewels when she'd been the one to find the clues. Cursing under her breath, she stalked into the dining room, immediately spotting him amongst the other few guests.

"What the hell are you doing here, James?"

He looked up from his paper, a pretty porcelain cup held daintily between his two fingers. "Cat. What a surprise to see you here. Will you not join me?"

"You're a real bastard. I can't believe you actually followed me here. Only you would stoop so low. Not that it surprises me after you stole my find and took credit for my work." Did he know about the jewels? Or did he suspect she was onto something and was hoping he could figure out enough to beat her to the punch.

"My dear, your recollection of events seems to be different from what actually happened." His smug smile only angered her further.

People were starting to stare—and it probably didn't help that she looked intent on committing murder.

"You keep telling yourself that, but people are starting to see past your lies. Before long, you'll only have the undergrads to con and seduce into your bed."

He leaned towards her, closing the distance between them so he was infuriatingly close. "It was a bed you were more than happy to share with me, my dear. Or have you forgotten all those lovely nights together?"

Her skin crawled at the memory. She had been stupid and naïve, but she was seldom a fool twice. "Why are you here? Or are you going to try and tell me it's just a coincidence that you've shown up in the same town I'm in—the same hotel—when you're a day's drive from home."

"I cannot help where my research takes me. Perhaps it is you who's following me? Why are *you* here?" He perked an eyebrow in question, making her want to wring his neck.

In her desperation to throw him off her track, the words were out of her mouth before she'd thought them through. "I'm here to visit my boyfriend, if you really must know. So don't waste your time, James. Go. Home."

She pulled herself upright, scoffed, and then walked away without another glance. By the time she got outside, her heart was pounding a deafening beat, and her body was shaking.

How the hell had he tracked her to Dunmuir? The only ones she'd told were the MacCraighs, since she was meeting with them, and Tansy, who'd nearly murdered James herself when that nastiness went down with her previous research project. He must have followed her when she first came up. Damn it!

And now that he'd caught whiff of a find? She'd never get rid of him—unless he actually believed she was here on a romantic getaway. What had come over her, she didn't know, but with luck, he might actually believe her and go back to Cambridge. In the meantime, she'd channel her anger into finding the necklace.

Before he got the chance to follow her to Iain's, she got in her car and headed off, going for a bit of a drive first to make sure he hadn't caught up to her. She'd need to find another place to stay too, though that would have to wait until after her meeting with Iain. It'd be impossible to avoid James if they were staying in the same inn. Problem was, in a place as small as Dunmuir and with the closest city nearly two hours away, she might be hard pressed to find a different place. Perhaps she could grab a room at a bed and breakfast, though she suspected many of them might not be available in the off season.

When she pulled down the drive to the MacCraigh castle—for what else could it really be called—she found Iain hanging around outside with Duncan, the two of them playing fetch. She pulled up next to his car and got out as Duncan rushed to her side in a full body wiggle. She gave his head a good scratch before turning to Iain, whose attention was elsewhere.

He tilted his head in the direction of her small spare tire. "Ye shouldn't be driving around on that thing. Ye'll only end up breaking down again."

"Yeah, I've got to get it fixed. Anyplace you'd recommend where they might be able to get it done quickly?"

Iain shrugged. "Guess that'd depend on whether he's got yer size tire in stock. If he has to order it, it could take a few days."

"I'll have to take my chances on the spare then. I have no other way of getting here."

"If that's all, I could always come and get ye." As if that settled the matter, he moved onto the next topic of conversation. "I went through some of our books last night—the old ones. Don't know what ye're looking for, but I set aside a few interesting things pertaining to the time period."

"I appreciate it."

Perhaps she'd been too harsh on him and they'd gotten off to a rocky start. It would be good to have his cooperation and knowledge of clan history and lore. So much was often passed down in stories rather than written down. Indeed, it was because of her Scottish grandmother and the tales she'd heard as a child that she'd become interested in the history of her ancestors.

"Well, don't go getting ahead of yerself, lass. The only way ye're going to get access to those books is if ye first tell me what yer looking for and why ye're really here."

"Look, I'm happy for any help you're willing to give me, but like I said, I need more information first. I'm not sure of things just yet, and it'd be premature to speculate." Why did it feel like they were constantly rehashing things? And here she'd gone thinking she'd judged him too harshly.

"No, my dear." He crossed his arms and stopped walking, his head cocked to the side with a smirk on his lips. "Ye tell me now, or ye can find whatever it is yer looking for without my help or my clan."

She was tempted to walk away. James had set her nerves on edge, she'd yet to have a cup a coffee, and she was in no mood to negotiate with Iain when Callum had ensured her of their cooperation.

So why was she was stuck dealing with a stubborn bastard like Iain instead of his sweet father? She wanted to turn and go, yet she knew she'd regret it the moment she did. It would leave the treasure—*her* find—vulnerable to bastards like James, and that wasn't a risk she was willing to take. Treasure hunters would catch whiff and it would all be over—they wouldn't care about the historical significance or what it would mean to the people of Scotland. No. They'd only care about pawning it off to the highest bidder.

"Iain, please. I can't risk this getting out. The vultures are already circling. I've done my best to keep it all a secret, but it only takes a single drop of blood to bring the sharks feeding. And they're hungry, damn it."

His smirk faded to a look of concern. "If ye're worried I'll tell others, I'll not. Ye have my word. But I need to know what's going on, especially if there are others looking for whatever it is ye're trying to find. I have my family to think of and I'll not jeopardize their safety."

Now she'd gone and worried him needlessly. James was a lot of things, but she couldn't see him stooping so low as to hurt anyone physically, not even for a treasure as great as The Highlander's Hope.

"It's not like that. It's a colleague—Dr. James Tanner—who wants to take credit for anything I find. He's done it before, and I'm afraid it's made me overly cautious."

"And can ye say for sure that there aren't others?"

Weariness had her letting out a long sigh. "No, I'm not sure. There could be other people looking for it, and they may very well be a hell of a lot more ruthless."

"And ye've brought that to my front door? I can't say I appreciate that, Dr. Ross."

Crap. What had she done? She looked deep into his sea blue eyes, their gaze intense. "I'm sorry. It's never been my intention to put anyone in danger. But I've been very careful, and I have to believe that no one knows what it is I'm looking for. Not even James."

"Get inside. We're going to sort this out right now." He glanced around as if expecting someone to be watching, and then with a hand on her shoulder, got her moving forward and towards the house.

Once indoors, she followed him down the hall to a portion of the home she'd not been in before. Portraits and weaponry hung on the dark wood paneled walls, while elaborate rugs covered the wide plank flooring, and the ceilings soared high above them. He took one turn and then another, winding around towards the back of the house. Finally, he pulled open a door, and let her step through.

Her heart pitter-pattered in delight at the sight of all the books, despite her recent troubles. Two levels of full-sized book cases lined every wall, the only interruption occurring where the stone fireplace cobbled its way to the ceiling. A roaring fire was already dancing in its confines as if in anticipation of their arrival, warding off the damp of the autumnal morning.

Iain stopped short and spun on her, her reveries over the books dissolving like smoke caught on a wind. "You need to tell me everything you know. Now."

His eyes locked on hers, his jaw stiff as he spoke. He was angry, but if he thought he could bully her, he'd soon find out just how wrong he was.

"Look, I don't mind sharing some information, but I can't tell you everything. This is bigger than all of us, and I can't risk letting it fall into the wrong hands. I'm here as a researcher, and I swear I'll do right by your family, but I need your support."

"I'm sorry, lass, but if ye want my support then ye need to trust me with what it is we're looking for. You've put my family in danger, and I'll be damned if I'm going to fumble around in the dark not knowing who or what will be coming. I want answers, Cat."

"Look… James might be an ass, but he wouldn't physically hurt anyone."

"Aye, this *James* seems the trustworthy sort from what ye've said of him. And what of the others? Can you be so sure of them?" He ran a rough hand through his thick chestnut locks.

Unfortunately, Iain was right, even if Cat was loath to admit it. "Then help me find it before the others figure out what we're up to."

He laughed while shaking his head. "I'd be happy to, lass—if ye'd tell me what the hell it is I'm actually trying to find. Tell me what it is we're looking for and ye can have access to all ye need, and I'll help in any way I can. But it's not going to happen if ye're keeping secrets from me—especially not when my family's involved."

She debated telling him she'd find a way without him, but there was no point to it. Especially not when James was on her trail. Iain had her cornered, and telling him the truth would be the only way to get him to cooperate.

"Fine. We can work together." Annoyance still crept into her voice, and she put little effort into trying to disguise it.

"Is it The Highlander's Hope?" When Cat cursed under her breath, he howled in excitement. "I knew it. I just knew it had to be."

He was grinning like the cat who'd stolen the cream, and she was irked to no end. "So now you know. Happy?"

"It's a start." He walked over to a desk, glancing over his shoulder to make sure she was following. "There's one more order of business. I need ye to sign this."

Cat picked up the papers and flipped through them, her eyes scanning the pages, her anger building with each word. "Are you kidding? You want me to sign a confidentiality agreement? You must think awfully highly of yourself."

"What I do think is that the tabloids are happy to get their hands on anything at all, and will pay handsomely for it. So you can either sign, or leave. The choice is yours."

"You're awfully good at ultimatums." She glared at him, but knew there was no point to protesting, and she had no interest in the tabloids, it didn't really matter. She grabbed a pen from his desk and quickly signed the papers, handing them back to him, none too gently. "I'm not here for gossip or to spy on you and your girlfriends."

"Just a small precaution is all." He motioned towards a stack sitting on an end table. "These are the books I mentioned. There are notes in some, and then there are also a few journals. I don't know where ye'd like to start or what ye're looking for, but I'm happy to help."

She took it as a truce. If he was willing to help her find the Hope, then that was all that mattered. Letting out a sigh, she let her anger go, happy to get back to the reason she was there and the only thing of any importance.

Her research had turned up a connection to the jewels few would know about, and even fewer would likely document openly, given the time period. The books Iain had gathered—especially the journals—might help to reinforce the information she'd found. And now that Iain had weaseled his way into her find, she'd make the most of his offer to help.

"I think the journals might be a good place to start, but first, I was wondering if you knew of any clan stories that were passed down through the generations. Given the importance of the jewels, I suspect they'd try to mask the clues in the spoken word rather than the written."

"My father would be the one to talk to about that—or our housekeeper, Mrs. Wallace. She would likely know the stories better than anyone, though she's only here once a week on Mondays."

"Should we go through the journals then?" Despite all the annoyances of the day, excitement bubbled within her like champagne drunk too fast, ecstatic to be looking for the necklace once more.

He leaned against the desk, his arms crossed in front of his chest, so his shirt stretched tight over his muscles. "Not yet, lass. If I'm going to be of any help to ye, I need to know what ye've already found."

And just like that—she felt like a soda gone flat.

She shook her head no, wondering how the hell this all got away from her so quick. "This is not your find, Iain, it's my research—research I've worked hard on. I truly appreciate your help with this, and I'll give you full credit for that, but it doesn't mean we're partners."

He lazily stretched out his long legs in front of him as if he hadn't a care in the world and shrugged, a smirk on his lips. "Ye see, I think it means *exactly* that. If the Hope necklace is found on my lands, then you can have full credit for finding it and analyzing the historical records that uncovered it, but the necklace will still be mine."

She forced herself to take a deep breath and calm down, so that she wouldn't lunge at his neck, wrap her fingers around it and strangle the life out of him. "Please, do *not* tell me you're going to hock that necklace to the highest bidder. You can't possibly sell the Hope when it has such historic importance. If you do, then you're an even bigger jerk than I first thought—and given the circumstances under which we met, that's saying something."

"Well, ye may think me a jerk and an idiot, but I take offence that ye'd think I'd sell something of such significance to my country and clan." He leaned forward so they were only inches away, anger ablaze in his eyes, but she refused to budge even if he was infuriatingly close. "I'm a highlander, aye? That necklace means more to me than you could ever know."

Cat racked her brain for the legal wording and specifics. "Well, you wouldn't be able to sell it anyway. Though the Treasure Act may not apply to Scotland, you still abide by *bona vacantia,* and that means the treasure itself would go to the National Museum, though you'd be paid its equivalent."

"Ah… but would it really?" His smirk was infuriating. "Ye've said ye have information that involves my clan and that my clan was in possession of it, no? And my understanding is that as long as there's a living descendent, the treasure belongs to that heir. Since my family is still in existence and the rightful heirs, the Highlander's Hope would remain ours."

His smug smile made her want to wipe it from his face. Her mind raced through the law's details, and though she couldn't come up with all the specifics, Iain would likely have a case in court.

She could only appeal to his honor. "Then I'm begging you, Iain. Do the right thing and keep it safe. Promise me you won't sell the Highlander's Hope."

"Only if ye give me yer word that ye'll stop being such a pain in my arse." He cocked his head, humor glinting in his eyes.

"Iain, I want your word. Promise me—or I swear, I won't be able to think straight."

He laughed and shook his head, his gaze locked on hers so her breath caught and her heart raced. His voice was gentle when he spoke. "Aye, lass. Whist. Ye have my word."

Relief overwhelmed her, as a smile tugged at her lips. "You're just lucky your clan isn't bigger. 'Cause there's no way in hell you'd be my first choice for a partner."

"Aye, the feeling's mutual, lass. Believe me… the feeling's mutual."

CHAPTER Four

I AIN LEANED IN to look at the notes Cat had scribbled in her notebook, curious about what had led her to the MacCraigh clan. Now that he was less worried about her snooping around his troubles, and he knew it really was the Hope they were looking for, it could very well be the financial lifeline he needed. He'd do his best to keep his promise to her, but he'd also do whatever was needed to keep his family safe. A heavy weight lifted off his chest, and though he was a long way from breathing easy, he could finally relax a bit.

He looked over at his new partner as she went through her notes. She was an interesting creature. Completely unlike any other woman he'd known. The girl was smart, of that there was no question. What he hadn't expected was the passion that sparked in those green eyes or the sarcasm and humor that laced her words—especially now that they'd finally sorted out their differences. Truth was, she was far too entertaining a distraction from his troubles. Maybe his father was right after all.

"It really was sheer luck that I found the clue. I'm sure you know of Lord George Murray, a commander to Prince Charles Stuart." When he nodded, she continued. "Do you know of his trusted friend and lieutenant, Robert Cameron?"

"Aye, it's rumored he had the necklace well before Culloden, but after that, the references to its whereabouts stop. No one knows where it ended up. There are no references to it, Cat." He leaned back, wondering if she'd gotten it all wrong. Surely others would have figured it out by now if there were clues out in the open.

"You're right. There are no references to it—at least not where one might expect to find them. My research actually started as a documentation of love letters during the time of the uprising. Trust me when I tell you, the last thing I expected to find were clues to the Highlander's Hope."

"In a love letter?" He supposed it was possible. "But hadn't historians already looked at the commanders and their families? One would think it'd show up."

She spun in her seat to face him, a knowing smile dancing upon her full lips. "They did look at their families. However, our dear Mr. Cameron, though loyal to Bonnie Prince Charlie, was a little less loyal to his wife. The love letter was to Nessa, his mistress. Very few knew about their relationship back then, and even fewer were aware of it with the passing of time."

Her smile was infectious, for he could now see how it may have all played out. "Cameron gave *her* the jewels."

"Exactly! He knew his family would come under scrutiny by the British, and didn't want the necklace to be found or for his family to be implicated. Since few knew about his mistress, she seemed the logical choice." Her excitement softened, and her eyes seemed distant, as if she'd been transported to a different time. "He loved her, and she loved him. Their trust was implicit and complete. He knew she wouldn't betray him—and don't you see? It was their love and trust that kept this priceless treasure safe all these years."

He had to smile at her dreamy-eyed romanticism. "And my clan? How was my family connected?"

"Nessa had been married and widowed. It was her husband—he was a MacCraigh. They had two sons together before his untimely death— they'd be your ancestors." She closed her notebook. "From what I can tell, her relationship with Robert didn't start until after she'd become widowed from John MacCraigh. I believe Robert and John had been good friends and once John passed away, Robert did his best to help his friend's widow and sons."

"Ah… and help the widow he did." It was starting to make sense.

"It wasn't like that, Iain." She shifted in her seat, her brows pulled in a furrow. "Nessa and Robert had been friends before she married, and they didn't become lovers for years after John's death."

Iain realized just how seriously she took all this. She was truly vested in these people's lives. He guessed it must happen when one did such extensive research. "I'd not meant to imply that she wasn't loyal to her husband."

"I know it doesn't really matter, but…" She sighed with a shrug.

"Aye, lass. I get it. Ye get to know them through their letters and looking into their lives. And it does matter. My apologies. I'd meant no disrespect." He gave her hand a quick squeeze, trying to reassure her that he truly meant the words he'd just spoken. Though they'd gotten off to a rocky start, he was happy the tension between them had eased. "Where did ye find the letters anyway?"

"The museum's library didn't have a whole lot of information on them. Only that they'd been found tucked away in a hidden compartment of a desk that was being reconditioned. Whoever found them thought they might be of historical significance and donated them."

He supposed some of his family's furnishings could have gotten sold off during less prosperous times or been given away as a form of payment. "What happened to the happy couple?"

"Robert died at Culloden. As for Nessa, she married soon after Robert's death, and quickly bore her husband a daughter."

Iain looked at her in question. "How quick?" The implied meaning wasn't lost on Cat.

"Quicker than most would have expected given the date of her marriage." She smiled at that, as if happy that Nessa was able to keep a part of Robert with her after his death.

A hopeless romantic. Iain had to smile at that. "Well then, we might as well get started."

"I have copies of the letters if you want to go through them. Might be a good idea, since you know your family history, and I could easily miss something, not thinking it important." She pulled a file from her bag and handed it to him. "Here. Just please, do *not* leave these hanging around. The fewer people who know about your family's connection, the better."

"And what of this guy ye're worried about? Does he know ye're after the necklace?" If there was an outside threat, then he needed to know just how serious it was.

"That would be Dr. James Tanner. He's a fellow historian, but he's also a bastard."

And a hell of a lot more, Iain thought, by the heat in her tone. "Does he know what ye've been researching?"

She shook her head no, though she didn't look convincing. "He hasn't made the connection yet, but he followed me up from Cambridge. Turned up in my hotel this morning, which is going to make it damn hard to come and go without him taking notice. Actually… I have a confession to make. And I swear, I would *never* do this sort of thing under any circumstance—except that I panicked."

"Cat. What did ye do?" A sliver of dread pierced his chest.

"I really am sorry." Her brows were drawn together, her eyes pleading with him for understanding.

"Cat."

She cringed and looked away. "I told him I was here to see my boy-friend—and if he happened to follow me here, then he'll think you're him. My boyfriend. *Crap!* I'm sorry. I don't even do relationships anymore, so don't think it's some sort of weird play for you just because you're Scotland's most eligible bachelor."

He swallowed the laugh that wanted to erupt. Now wasn't that one hell of a corner Little Miss Librarian had just backed herself into. Not that he'd be letting her out of it just yet.

"I'm not sure I believe ye, love." He watched her eyes go wide as she stammered in shock, looking deliciously mortified. "Ye wouldn't be the first to try tricking me into bed for a shag, love. Though I'll admit, I hadn't really been expecting it from ye."

To say her face had gone red would be an understatement, and it utterly delighted him. "You can't possibly think I'm trying to *sleep with you*. Of all the absurd things. I've never..."

"Never?" He feigned mock horror, and then burst out laughing. "I'm kidding. Ye're fine, love. I understand why ye did it, and truth is, it's a believable excuse—as long as we're able to convince everyone of it. If we can't, then he'll know ye're hiding a far bigger secret."

"You're such a jerk. I can't believe you did that to me." She swatted at him and then collapsed back on the sofa. "And I need a new place to stay, or I'm liable to murder James—and you too, while I'm at it."

"Ye'll be staying here. Remember? You're my girlfriend now, and I'm not going to risk having others find out about the necklace just because one of your exes is snooping around."

"I never said he was my ex, Iain." Suspicion had her glaring at him.

"Calm yerself, lass—a blind man could tell there was something be-tween the two of ye and it all went wrong. I've no interest in yer relations or where ye lay yer head at night, except for the fact that this now involves me and mine and I need to keep them safe. People get crazy when a treasure's involved, and the last thing we need is others catching wind of this." Better to be paranoid and safe. "We've plenty of room here, and it'll make it easier for us to work together."

"What about James?"

"Ye made yer bed, love. And what a nice bed it'll be with the two of us sharing it." He leaned in and brushed her cheek, a laugh bursting forth when she pursed her lips in annoyance and slapped his hand away. "Besides, even if ye told him ye were researching something completely unrelated, he'd still linger to see what ye'd find. But our little ruse should do the trick. Even if ye split ages ago, no man wants to see his ex with another. He'll not be able to take it for long."

"Then why didn't I just stay here to start with? He's already seen me at the inn, Iain. He must suspect something's up." She went back to being panicked. "And it's not like we look like lovers. We've argued every time we've met, and James may be an ass, but he's not an idiot. He'll see right through it."

"Will he?" Iain leaned in, his gaze soft but unwavering, his eyes locked on hers as he tucked a curl behind her ear, his fingers lingering as he took a deep breath, her scent filling his head. She blushed like a girl after her first kiss, and he had to laugh, his little experiment over. "It will work, aye? But only if ye don't go red every time I touch ye or slap me away."

"Well, what do you expect? I'm supposed to be here for research, not a romp."

"Don't go worrying that pretty little head of yers—I'll think ye no less professional if ye relax a bit and pretend to enjoy my company." By the gods, the woman could drive a man to drink. "As for why ye were at the inn, we'll make sure he overhears my excuse of getting caught out of town on business and my apologies that it forced ye to stay at the inn."

It could work. Hell, it had to. In a small village like Dunmuir, a rumor of any treasure, let alone the Highlander's Hope, would spread like wildfire, especially if this James fellow started to openly question Cat's motives where others could overhear.

She shook her head, her lips pursed and worry tainting her eyes. "I don't know, Iain…"

"Come." He stood and grabbed her hand, hauling her to her feet.

"Where the hell are we going?" He got drawn brows and a scowl from her. She was interesting—and hard-headed to boot. This could be fun.

"First things first." He spun her around and pulled out the large clip that held her long curls in place. It tumbled down over her shoulders as she futilely protested and he ran his fingers through her hair.

"What the hell, Iain?"

Refusing to let her ruin their plan, he wrapped an arm around her waist and pulled her close, their bodies pressed together. "Ye want this to work, right? Then we're going to wander through town, pretending to be lovers, before we go back to yer hotel to grab yer things. And no clips—my women wear their hair down."

She stammered and cursed as he laughed. By the gods, this was going to be fun.

Once in town, Iain and Cat walked into the pub hand in hand, and took a seat by the window, knowing they'd need to lay the groundwork to make their relationship believable. He could tell she was still uncomfortable with the role she was playing, but knew most wouldn't notice the slight tension in her body when her eyes still sparkled in his direction, and a sultry smile tugged at her lips.

He knew the rumors would be flying. Gossip was easily the most popular pastime in Dunmuir, and this news would go the rounds faster than lice through a schoolyard. Though there were several places to get lunch, the pub was the most popular, especially with the locals. Busy as it was, it wouldn't take long for word to get out that Iain MacCraigh, confirmed bachelor and local laird, was getting intimate with a pretty brunette. Though he dated plenty, he seldom brought anyone home to Dunmuir—and that alone would be enough to get the rumor mill churning.

"The daily menu's there on the board, love." He gave her a seductive smile and linked his hand with hers across the table, knowing all eyes in the pub were on them.

They chatted about nothing of importance, flirting and smiling their way through ordering and their meal. She was doing a good job of hiding any awkwardness she felt, the only sign of it in the occasional widening of her eyes each time he pushed the flirting to the next step. No one could see it but him, and frankly he liked to put her on edge, liked to make her heart race.

A man Iain had never seen before approached their table, and the way he was eyeballing himself and Cat, it had to be James.

"Cat, what a pleasant surprise. I hadn't expected to find you here."

Any unease that may have been present in Cat's demeanor was now gone. As if not wanting to pull her attention away from Iain, she lazily turned towards her ex, her seductive smile quickly fading as she let out a weary sigh. "Why are you here, James? Are you now stalking me when I come to visit Iain? It's a bit much, don't you think?"

James gave Iain a quick once over before straightening his back and puffing out his chest. "Iain, is it?"

"Aye, it is. Cat, is this man bothering ye then?" Iain glared at James. "Cause I won't have anyone giving ye unwelcomed attentions."

She reached across the table and linked her fingers with his, her gaze soft and seductive, looking at him as if he was the only one in the world who mattered. Though he knew she was only playacting, it made his heart race to have her look at him that way.

When she spoke, her voice was like a heady port, rich and sweet, her gaze lingering upon him like a lover's touch. "Don't worry, my love. He's of absolutely no consequence, and I do believe he was leaving." She turned to James, her eyes hard as glass. "Weren't you?"

James looked from Iain to Cat and back, his lips curling in an ugly snarl. "No, as a matter of fact, I wasn't leaving. We have unfinished business to deal with, Cat."

Cat just laughed. "Yes, you never were any good at completing the task at hand, but you need not worry. Iain takes *very* good care of me, and nothing is ever left unfinished."

James went red, stammered a response he never managed to get out, and left, bumping into several people on his way out the door.

"Bloody hell, woman. Remind me never to anger ye—again." He looked at her with a whole new respect.

"Shall we go get my things, then?" She ran her hand up his arm, continuing her act with a new found confidence.

"Aye, love. I do believe our work here is done."

By the time Iain got her settled in one of the guest rooms, his father had returned from his bird-watching. "How was it then? See anything of interest?"

His father tossed his vest on the back of the sofa and took a seat, his brows drawn in annoyance. "Ne'er mind the birds, son. What is this I hear about ye having a new lass? Mrs. McGillis said she'd ne'er seen two people looking more in love. I'm nothing but happy at the prospect that ye've found someone, but next time, I'd rather hear it from yer mouth rather than another's. Caught me off guard."

Iain sighed, not wanting to disappoint his father, who wanted to see him settled with a wife and family. "Da, it was just a ruse. What I'm about to say, ye can't repeat to anyone—not to Mrs. Wallace, nor my brother or sister."

"Ye have me worried now, lad."

"I'll not tell ye there's no reason to worry, but all is well for now. It's Cat, Da. She's looking for the Highlander's Hope and thinks there's a good chance it's on our lands."

Slack-jawed, his father sat back, the color draining from his face. "I can't believe it."

"That's the reason we were about town as a couple. One of her colleagues followed her to Dunmuir, and we can't have anyone thinking she's here on a treasure hunt. No one can know what we're up to. It could get dangerous if anyone found out."

"Where's the lass now? I hope ye've not left her on her own if there's trouble brewing."

"She's staying here, if that's all right? Getting settled in upstairs, as we speak. We need to keep up impressions, and it seemed to be the best way to work together on finding the necklace and keep everyone safe."

"Of course she should stay. And I promise to not say anything to anyone." Callum shook his head, a smile springing to his lips. "The Highlander's Hope. I can't believe it. And she's sure?"

"It looks like there's a good chance." He returned his father's smile, happy to not have him worrying. "One more thing. I think it best ye go and visit Malcolm or Moira. Just for a little while until we have a better idea of what we're up against."

"Ye always did worry too much, though I'll go if it'll keep ye happy." He got to his feet and grabbed his vest. "But ye better treat the lass with respect."

"Aye, Da. Ye have my word."

CHAPTER Five

WHILE CAT REVIEWED the journals Iain had set aside, he went through the letters she'd collected. She jotted notes and took photos of the pages with her phone. It was a quick and easy way to maintain access to the original texts, especially when she often had to return them.

They were once more in the library, sprawled out on either end of the large sofa with their reading material in hand, and a cup of tea within reach. They had been at it for hours, and the tea was doing little to keep her going.

The rush of adrenaline she'd gotten from running into James had worn off. She still couldn't believe they'd pulled it off. The whole thing was so unlike anything she'd ever done before. And her snarky response to James? Tansy would have been whooping for joy had she been there.

It left her feeling empowered, especially after what he'd done to her. It even seemed to have eased some of the tension between her and Iain. Maybe their arguments would be a thing of the past, now that they were finally working towards a common goal.

"Anything in the letters?" Cat kept hoping Iain would come across a section laced with hidden meaning, and would understand it for what it was, given it was his clan's history.

"Nothing yet." Iain sat up from where he'd been hunched over reading, running a rough hand through his thick locks and down his face. With his face cast in shadow, his mussed-up hair, and the dark stubble on his chin, she could see him as a highlander of old, his ancestors' blood running strong.

"I need to get up and move around. Clear my head." Cat stood and stretched, her head going lightheaded for a moment.

"Come on then. It's too late to go out, but this place is large enough to wander around in. Ye might even find it interesting."

Cat followed him out of the library and down the corridor. From what she'd seen of the exterior, it was obvious they weren't using the house in its entirety. As with many ancient homes, upkeep was often difficult and costly, leaving many to close off the sections not in use or in disrepair.

"I'm driving my father to Edinburgh first thing in the morning, so he can stay with my brother. Thought ye might want to come along." Iain guided her through a door.

"I wouldn't want to be a bother." They turned down another corridor and then down a flight of stairs.

"No bother at all. My father's quite fond of ye, and it'd keep me from worrying about ye alone in this house." Iain held open a door for her, and they stepped into a massive room that likely served as a ballroom once upon a time.

"You mean you don't want me to find the necklace while you're gone, and run off with it?" Though she was only kidding, she wondered if it was closer to the truth than she'd like.

He spun on her, closing the distance between them, his arm wrapping around her waist before she had a chance to react, his lips curling like a hunter who's found his prey. "No. If I'd meant that, then that's what I would've said. And if the necklace were so easy to find, do ye not think my clan would have already stumbled across it? And here I was worried about ye."

She looked up at him, but he was so close it had her heart stumbling over itself. It took all she had to force her voice to be steady. "I was kidding."

"Were ye?"

She pulled out of his arms and turned away, not quite sure what the hell was going on between them. It'd be hard to deny she felt a certain attraction to him, but she had no time for that sort of thing, and she'd too recently gotten burned by allowing her love life to interfere with her work.

Not wanting the awkwardness to linger between them and make it difficult to work together, she tried her best to move past it. "Edinburgh sounds lovely, if you don't mind me tagging along."

It would feel too awkward to be in their home when they weren't there—not to mention it could open her up to liabilities and headaches she didn't need. The last thing she needed was for someone to accuse her of taking the Hope while they were away. Not that Iain or his father would do such a thing, but... better to be safe.

"I wouldn't have offered if I didn't want ye to join me." He shook his head, grabbed her hand, and started walking towards the door at the far end of the large room.

"Where are we going?" Tall as Iain was and with the pace he was suddenly keeping, Cat had to hustle to keep up with him. "And would you please slow your ass down? I'm only five three."

"For a Ph. D., ye certainly have a mouth on ye." His pace slowed at least, though he'd yet to let go of her hand or stop.

"Are we just wandering about then? Or is there a point to you dragging me around?"

With pursed lips, he gave her a quick glare. "I remembered something and want to check it out. Mind ye, I haven't been in this portion of the home since I was a kid, so I'm not quite sure what to expect."

A few more rooms and long corridors, and they entered another large chamber. The temperature was cooler here by several degrees, and the lighting was now nothing more than a bare bulb barely throwing off enough light to fight back the darkness. Dust clothes draped over amorphous mounds, leaving the room cluttered with mysteries waiting to be uncovered.

"When they closed off the rest of the home, or some rooms became too damaged to repair, anything of importance was brought here to keep it protected. I remember there being several paintings, some of them portraits. We have the journals and the letters, but it could be they hid clues there also."

Her body tensed with excitement as it occurred to her how right he may be. "It's actually a brilliant idea to think of the paintings, especially when few could read back then."

"Aye, not to mention it'd be easier for a book or letter to get lost." He wandered around the room looking at the various mounds as if deciphering what was hidden underneath. "Here, give me a hand."

She moved to the opposite side of the pile he was standing at, and together they lifted the covering, sending up a cloud of dust. Several chairs and small tables huddled together. They draped the cloth back over the items and moved to the next grouping with the hope they'd get lucky. After striking out a few more times, they hit pay dirt. Propped against the wall were several paintings, each wrapped further for additional protection.

"These are them." Iain picked up a few of the smaller paintings, setting aside the larger ones for himself. "Can ye carry these? We'll take them back to the library."

Cat grabbed hold of the paintings he handed her. "We might need to make a few trips."

'*A few trips*' was an understatement. By the time they finished, she was covered in dust and in horrible need of a shower, though that'd have to wait. She was desperate to look at the paintings.

Iain started to uncover them. "There was one painting in particular. It was the portrait of a woman—don't remember the period of it, but I know it was quite old. I'm now wondering if it could be Nessa MacCraigh—or her daughter."

Cat turned on a few more lights, excited to see what clues might be tucked away between the brushstrokes. "Unless it's blatantly obvious, I think it'll be up to you to pick out any clues hidden in the paintings, since you'd be more familiar with them."

Iain unwrapped the last painting and let out a sigh, his shoulders slumping. "The one I was thinking of—it's not here. My father might know where it is, though right now he's out with his friends having a pint and playing cards."

"We can always go through these and then head back and look through the remaining piles. I'm sure it's still there." She could tell he was frustrated. "Look… it takes time to comb through the information and details. It really is like trying to find a needle in a haystack. You just need to be more patient."

"Let's just say I've ne'er been the patient sort."

All too anxious to see what might be found, she'd been lingering over his shoulder to look at the paintings as he uncovered them. So when he stood and turned, she found herself face to face with him, their bodies all but brushing together, the air between them suddenly charged with energy. His eyes took her in with an intensity that made her think she knew all too well what it must feel like when a wolf catches sight of its prey.

And then just like that he moved away, leaving her to finally exhale and get control of her racing heart.

He was already heading for the door. "Look over the paintings. I'll be back in a bit."

Duncan looked between the two of them, and then, deciding the spot in front of the fire was better than running around a cold castle, plunked his head back down and closed his eyes.

Happy to look for new clues, Cat turned her attention to the items they'd brought back. Most of the paintings were of landscapes, probably of the surrounding area. There were a few portraits, but based on the clothing, they were at least a hundred years past the dates they were interested in. Still, years of research taught her to be thorough. Nothing should be dismissed until it had been looked over carefully.

She started with the landscapes, but found nothing hidden amidst the trees and glens. There were no necklaces dangling from tree branches, or shimmering in the waters of the loch. The portraits were a similar disappointment. Cat hoped Iain was having better luck tracking down the paintings he was interested in. She waited a while longer and then debated going to give him a hand, in case he'd found more paintings than he could carry.

Having made the trip a few times with Iain, she thought she could find her way back to the room where everything was stashed, but she only it made it as far as the hall when she heard a knock at the front door.

She groaned. Answer it or ignore it? Iain was on the other side of the castle and would never hear the knocking, and his father was out for the evening.

The knocking turned to pounding. She approached the door, but there was no peephole, and there were no windows flanking the door to look out of. Shouting could be heard, but damned if she could make out a word through the thick oak and stone walls. How the hell did someone know whether or not to answer the door?

And then she found out.

Iain pulled her to the side, a shotgun in his hand and at the ready as he unlocked the door, turned the latch, and then stepped to the side, aiming at who might come in.

The man walked in, and immediately flinched at the gun pointed at his head. "Bloody hell, Iain. What the hell are ye trying to do to me? I just about had a coronary."

Iain lowered the shotgun, looking relieved. "Angus. I hadn't been expecting ye. Sorry."

Angus still looked at Iain with confusion, but any conversation was interrupted by Duncan launching himself at Angus with a full body wiggle. The dog got a good scratch but it was short lived given the shotgun and confusion.

"Angus, this is Cat; Cat, this is my dearest friend and cousin, Angus— and no, he's not a MacCraigh, in case ye were wondering." As if he'd let her ditch him to go find the jewels with a different clan member.

"It's a pleasure." Angus shook her hand, but then turned to Iain, his eyes narrowed and his head cocked to the side as if scrutinizing his friend's every move. "Ye've yet to explain why ye're toting a gun, and ne'er mind the rumors going about town."

"The rumors?" When Angus glanced in Cat's direction with those bright blue eyes of his, Iain gave her a sweet smile, and linked his hand with hers, bringing it to his lips. "I've no reason to deny them."

"They're true?" Angus turned a scrutinizing gaze on the couple before him, a single eyebrow perked and his eyes wide, disbelief in the tone of his voice.

"Bloody hell, man. Don't go looking at us like that. We met when I was away on business. I didn't say anything because it's been a bit of a long distance thing, and I wasn't sure how we'd manage it. But I'm happy to say, we've found a way to make it work." Iain's loving eyes took her in, and damn if he wasn't a good liar. Whether or not they'd fool Angus, however, was another question—especially if she was involved. Lying was *not* one of her strong suits, and the way Iain was looking at her had her pulse racing and her cheeks flaming hot.

"Well then, it's an absolute pleasure to meet ye. I didn't think Iain would ever bring anyone home. He must be... smitten." Nope. Angus still didn't look like he believed them, but he was a good enough sport to not question them openly.

"Did ye come by for anything in particular? I hadn't been expecting ye." Iain set the safety and put the shotgun down on a nearby table.

"Hadn't heard from ye, and figured I'd stop by, especially given the talk around town. Didn't realize ye had company. My apologies for interrupting."

Iain waved away his concerns. "Ye know ye're always welcome, and there's nothing to interrupt. Join us for a whisky?"

"I could do with a drop." Angus was still watching their every move, making Cat feel as if every breath, every beat of their heart was under scrutiny.

They wandered into the sitting room and Iain went to get them a whisky, while she and Angus grabbed a seat. He was tall—really tall—and definitely a looker, with black unruly locks and piercing blue eyes. Add to that the scruffy casual look, and she was sure he had every woman within a twenty-mile radius swooning.

Too bad he was making her panic.

Trying to distract Angus from his suspicions, and to keep herself from bolting, Cat tried a bit of small talk. "So, did you guys go to school together?"

"Aye, we did. Grew up together, given that our mothers were sisters. And what about the two of ye? Tell me about this whirlwind romance." The shit eating grin on his face was just more confirmation that he didn't believe a word they'd said.

"We met after he nearly ran me over while I attempted to fix my flat tire." Was her voice sounding high? Or was she only sounding panicked in her own head? At least she'd stuck to the truth—for now.

Angus burst out laughing, easing the tension knotting her muscles. "Now that I can believe. He drives like the hounds of hell are chasing him."

"Hey! I'm right here." They ignored Iain's protests.

Feeling a bit more at ease, Cat launched into her story, making up the rest of it as she went along. "At least he was nice enough to drive me home, since the walk to Cambridge would've taken me half the day. To repay him for his kindness, I bought him dinner."

Iain handed them each a drink, and then sat by her side, wrapping an arm around her shoulder with a smile. "And then I bought us drinks, hoping I'd have enough time to convince her to see me again."

"Well, I'm happy to hear it then." Angus tilted his head in Cat's direction. "I'll have ye know, he's not brought anyone home since secondary school. It'll be good for him to get away from his work and actually enjoy himself a bit."

She liked Angus, and was now feeling guilty that they were lying to him. Yet they had to, so she steeled herself to continue their charade. Trying to act as natural as possible, she twined her fingers with Iain's and leaned towards him with a smile she hoped didn't look stiff, as her gaze lingered on his handsome face while snuggling up to him. "I think it's been a good thing for both of us."

"Aye, lass. Ye both look happy." Angus gave her a sweet smile that reached his eyes this time, letting her breath a small sigh of relief. He then turned to his best friend, the sweet smile gone. "Now are ye going to tell me what's up with the shotgun? I've ne'er seen ye so jumpy before."

Cat looked at Iain in question, wondering if he'd manage to lie successfully. If it were her, she knew she'd have a hard time convincing anyone who truly knew her. A good thing James had never bothered to pay attention to anyone but himself.

Iain shrugged. "Cat has an ex that followed her up from Cambridge. I just didn't like the look of him is all. Thought I'd scare him off. The gun wasn't even loaded."

Angus looked to Cat. "Is that true?"

"That I have a jerk of an ex, and he showed up in town? Unfortunately, though he's not dangerous. The gun was a bit of overkill." Cat tossed Iain a scolding glance, playing things up for Angus.

Though the gun was over the top, the stakes were high and there was a lot to be lost. She hated to admit it for even a second, but people had killed for less—and this was the Highlander's Hope. She could see why Iain was being overly cautious, even if she still thought they were safe since no one really knew what they were after.

Angus looked at the two of them, and shook his head. "All right. I'll let it go for now."

"Will ye stay for a bit of dinner?" Iain sat forward.

Angus stood, finished his drink, and set the glass aside. "No. I should go. But if ye need anything, call me. Promise." His gaze was direct, locked on Iain's, his tone serious.

"Aye, I promise."

CHAPTER
Six

"I FOUND IT." IAIN wandered down the hall and grabbed the painting from where he stashed it when he'd heard the pounding at the front door.

Taking it back to the library, he uncovered it. It was like he remembered—the beautiful woman gazing mournfully out the window of the sitting room, the hills stretching out just beyond. She was stunning, her porcelain skin glowing with a blush across high cheekbones, her blue eyes contrasting with her deep brown hair.

Cat leaned in close to take a look, so he shifted a bit to make room her, all too aware of her body brushing against his. "There doesn't seem to be anything obvious, though I wouldn't really expect there to be. They wouldn't want to call attention to anything too obvious."

"The room she's in… it's our sitting room. I recognize the landscape shown in the window, and the detail of the wood paneling is the same." He looked again, taking in the details.

Her dress was modest, though the details of the gown and the rich burgundy brocade spoke of a certain status. A sheer lace covered her from neck to chest, though there were no other adornments. No necklace flashing like a beacon.

"That painting there." Cat pointed to it in the portrait, where it hung on the wall behind the woman. "I've seen it."

She moved to where they'd propped the other pieces of art, and started looking through them. "Right here."

She brought it over and propped it next to the portrait.

"Aye. So?"

"I don't know, now do I?" She glared at him before turning her attention back to the matter at hand. "The clue could be anything—a single brushstroke, a spark of light, a misplaced vase."

"Or nothing at all. We could be trying to find something where nothing exists." He hated to be the realist, but it seemed she was always far too hopeful where the jewels were concerned. Maybe it was the romantic in her. She just couldn't give up on the lovers, as if finding the Hope would somehow bring their love full circle.

"That's true. There could be nothing at all, or it could be right in front of us."

He stood up and stretched. "I'm starving, and if I don't eat something soon, I'm going to get grumpy."

"Please, then, don't let me stop you. 'Cause you know you've been an absolute joy up until now, and I'd hate to be the reason for your souring mood."

The smile that tugged at her lips and the humor that danced in those green eyes sparked something primal in him. By the gods, she made it so he couldn't think rationally. "Come. Ye need to eat."

"Do I?" She crossed her arms and cocked her head. "You're so incredibly bossy."

"Bossy, aye? Perhaps, but I'd rather be bossy than stubborn."

She shrugged and tilted her head, her brow perking in a dare. "I'm only stubborn when I'm right."

He had to laugh. "Then ye must think yerself right an awful lot, since ye're the most stubborn lass I've e'er met."

"I am not." She scowled.

"Ye're right. Ye're not." He threw his hands up in surrender.

She pursed her lips together with eyes narrowed, as if trying to figure out whether or not she should be angry with him. He just had to laugh.

"Come. My da will tan my hide if he finds out I let ye starve." With a hand on her back, Iain gently got her moving and steered her towards the door, not surprised when Duncan trotted past them in the hopes of a stray morsel, his ESP for all things food-related kicking into overdrive.

He showed her through to the kitchen, flicking on the lights in the large room. He'd renovated the space just a few years back when the economy was good and his investments were bringing in a nice return. They were still doing relatively well, but to avoid taking a hit with the tumbling economy, he'd tied up most of his funds, leaving him unable to sort out the current troubles his brother had caused.

Iain went to the large stainless fridge and opened the door, poking around to see what he could whip up. "Please tell me ye're not a vegetarian."

"I used to be."

"Why am I not surprised? Good thing ye came to yer senses." He flicked a glance over his shoulder, while pulling out some spicy Spanish sausage, an onion and pepper, a couple of potatoes, a chunk of cheese and a dozen eggs.

"I'm going to ignore that." She gave him a hand with the ingredients he was carrying. "Can I help you cook?"

"Depends. Can ye cut the sausage and pepper without chopping off a finger?" His brow perked in question as he got out a couple of knives and cutting boards. "Cause if ye end up needing stitches, we'll have to get Angus back here to sew ye up."

She took a board, a knife and the sausage, and started slicing it. "Is Angus a doctor then?"

"Closest doctor's an hour away. Angus is our local vet." He eyed her knife skills and guessed she'd done a fair amount of cooking. He grabbed a pan and put it on the burner, tossing a bit of oil in to heat up while he chopped the potatoes.

"The local vet, huh? I guess he'd do in a pinch." She smiled at him. "He was awfully nice, but I don't think he bought the whole couple thing."

"No, he didn't, though he won't say anything. He knows well enough that if I'm keeping something from him, I've got my reasons and I'll tell him when I'm ready." He tossed the thin slices of potatoes into the oil and then started on the onion. "Tell me more about James and what happened between the two of ye. I need to know if he believed us, or if he's going to be snooping around and causing trouble."

She shrugged, her knife cuts now coming down with far more intensity. "Even if he believed we're a couple, it won't make a difference to him if he thinks I may be looking for something. As for what happened between us, that's none of your business."

He bit down on the words that wanted to erupt forth, and tossed the onions into the oil, giving it all a quick stir. He took a deep breath and tried to keep the heat from his voice, annoyed that she was still keeping things from him. "It *is* my business as long as we're working together to find the jewels. Now start talking."

"No." Chop. Chop. Chop.

"Cat." He ignored the thrum of frustration winding itself through the very fiber of his being.

"Iain." More chopping.

The sausage was now in bits. He covered her knife hand with his so she'd stop hacking at the pieces, and then scooped up the meat and set it aside. "You need to tell me, Cat. I'm serious."

"And I'm serious about not telling you. My life—private and professional—is none of your business. He's not violent, if that's your concern. What he is, is an ass, and if you want more than that, you'll have to ask him yourself." She picked up the knife and started cutting the meat again, all while glaring at him.

He saw it coming, yet he couldn't get the words out fast enough to stop her. She sliced right into her finger as he watched. Her curses died on her lips as she sucked in air, pain lining her face as she cringed.

"Here. Give me yer hand." He grabbed a towel, and quickly wrapped it around her finger, applying as much pressure as possible while guiding her into a chair, as he kneeled in front of her.

"Blasted thing hurts. Let me see."

"Give it another minute." Ignoring how tight her shoulders looked, he tried not to panic. Why was it the bloody woman insisted on trying to get herself killed whenever in his presence? Good thing it was just her finger and not her wrist or gut. He steeled himself for the worst and got ready to take a look at it. "Ye're not going to pass out, are ye?"

"*No*. Are you?" Her eyebrows perked in question.

He pursed his lips in response, wondering how someone so mild-looking could be so incredibly annoying. Pulling back the cloth, he cringed at the long gash running across her finger. Luckily, it didn't look too deep, though after just a heartbeat, it was bleeding again. He covered it back up and applied pressure once more.

"It doesn't look like ye'll need stitches, but it's yet to stop gushing." With her hand still in his, he pressed down hard. He worried he was hurting her, her face looking more pale than before. "Are ye all right?"

She nodded. "Your potatoes. They're going to burn."

He took her other hand and placed it over her cut. "Apply pressure. If we can't get it to stop bleeding, I'll have to get Angus back over here to stitch it closed."

"Lovely."

He pulled the potatoes and onions from the oil, draining them on paper towels, and then grabbed another pan and got the rest of the ingredients going. There wasn't any blood to clean, but he cleared her board, and tossed it into the sink along with her knife. He felt guilty that she'd gotten hurt—especially since he was the one who'd been antagonizing her. The least he could do is keep her from starving.

Whisking a dozen eggs, he combined all the ingredients, topped it with some crumbled cheese and threw it into the oven. To keep Duncan from drooling onto the floor, he tossed the pup a chunk of sausage, finished cleaning up and then turned back to Cat.

"I'll be right back. I need to get you a bandage." He wandered down the hall and headed for the bathroom, when he thought he heard something in the library. Duncan was still in the kitchen, but maybe… "Da? Are ye back?"

Nothing. He changed direction, and went to investigate. It all looked the way they'd left it—or so he thought, since he hadn't exactly been paying attention to the exact placement of things. He went to the large casement windows that overlooked the stone patio and flicked on the outdoor lights. It all seemed normal, and yet… something seemed off.

The flower box in front of the window—it was no longer hanging where it should, but rather knocked to the ground, the soil and plants scattered. And there—wet footprints tracked across the pavers from the damp grass. The window had been locked though, so they hadn't made it in.

Or had they? The doors and windows—were they all locked?

Cat.

He raced to the kitchen, bursting into the room and quickly taking it all in, his heart thundering in his ears. "Are ye all right?"

"I'm fine. What's happened?" Her eyes went wide with alarm, as she got to her feet and came to his side.

"Someone was at the library window. They may have tried to get in, though I don't know for sure. Stay here. I've got to check the doors and windows. Make sure everything's locked." By the gods, it'd be close to impossible to check every window and door, especially in the older parts of the manor.

"I want to come with you."

He wanted to groan and tell her to stay put, but knowing how long he might stand there arguing with her, he gave in. "Come on then."

They started with the first floor, in the portion of the home they were still living in. It all seemed secure, though once more, they found footprints outside several more of the windows.

"I think they were just snooping around, and the main part of the house is locked up." Iain nodded towards her hand. "Let's get that finger seen to. I can check out the older parts of the home once we get that settled."

He thought she looked shaken, and if he had any doubt, her silence was enough to tell him he wasn't wrong. He grabbed the box of bandages and ointment, and sat her down, taking her hand in his. "Let's take a look."

The bleeding looked like it'd stopped. He gently squeezed some antibiotic ointment onto her cut, and then carefully bandaged it, making sure there was enough pressure applied to the wound to keep the cut from reopening while still allowing for proper circulation.

"Looks like you've done this before."

"Aye, well, I usually took care of my brother's scrapes when he didn't want my parents finding out he'd gotten himself into trouble." Clearly, not much had changed. "I'm going to take care of the rest of the house. I think whoever it was is long gone, but if you could draw the curtains in the library and get settled there, I'll not be long."

He took off and headed to the kitchen, pulling out his frittata just in the nick of time. With the oven off, he then locked down the rest of the home. The feeling of being watched made him angry, and left him feeling violated. Truth was, he was worried. Other than his brother's recent troubles, he'd never had reason to worry about his family's safety before, and it wasn't a feeling he was comfortable with. Though he might be overly paranoid, it didn't take a genius to know people had killed for a lot less than a bejeweled necklace of legend.

He called his father on his mobile phone, and told him to stay with his friends for the night, reassuring him that all was well. And it was. Everything was locked and secured, the curtains drawn. There was nothing to worry about. Or so he hoped.

He served up dinner, grabbed a couple of beers, and headed to the library.

"Here ye go." She thanked him, while he set her food down on the side table and then took a seat next to her on the sofa. "The doors and windows are locked, though anyone who really wants to get in can, given that the windows aren't barred."

"A comforting thought." She forked a piece of frittata into her mouth, and then looked up him, eyes wide. "This is *really* good."

"Ye sound shocked." He ate a bit of his own and then, uncapping the beers, handed her one, before taking a long pull of his own.

"I hadn't really expected you to know how to cook, is all. And certainly didn't think the food would be amazing."

"Amazing, aye? I'll take it." He gave her a sideways glance and a smile.

Settling back, he continued eating while looking at the paintings they had propped up across from the sofa. The woman in the painting was beautiful, but was it Nessa? He had to wonder if she even left any clues behind. Nessa may have told a select few in confidence, but would she risk the information and the necklace being lost, especially when those times were precarious and those taken into her confidence could easily perish? He doubted it. She would've had some sort of backup.

Once they finished their meal, he got back to the matter of who'd been snooping around. "Since that was likely James peeping at the windows, I think it's time ye told me about him—and what transpired between the two of ye."

She let out a huff of annoyance. "Fine. He's a colleague at the university. We were working together on a research project." She sighed and he sensed there was more to the story.

"So ye fell in love?" He could see it. The long hours spent in each other's company, shared interests.

"I wouldn't say that. In my experience, love is for fairytales and fools—or at the very least, other people. Just not me."

"Have ye ne'er been in love then?" She shrugged in answer to his question. "I can't believe it, lass. Or did some arse break yer heart?"

"I'll discuss James, since he's likely the one snooping around, but I'm not discussing my love life. Besides, you'd be bored to tears."

Bored, eh? Why did he like that she hadn't had much of a love life? "Fine. James then."

"We're both at the same department, and were collaborating on a project that overlapped. Long nights comparing notes, and we eventually started dating—until he went and published my research under his name, save for a brief footnote." Those last words were spoken through a stiff jaw.

"Was there no evidence to back up yer claim?" There had to be a way she could prove the work was hers.

"There would have been, except that he deleted my files from my laptop and school computer. With our research overlapping, he had enough information gathered to make a convincing argument." She took a deep breath that looked forced and then let it out slowly.

"He really is a bastard." Iain shook his head, annoyed. What sort of person would do that? "That he'd go as far as wiping yer files from yer hard drives... And I'm assuming he left behind no clues that it'd been him."

"No. Not that the board really looked too deep when one of their esteemed professors was involved. He knew exactly what he was doing—likely from the start." She bit her lip and then took a long swig from her beer, quiet for a bit before talking again. "I think that's the worst part of it. That he played me for a fool from the very beginning, and I was stupid enough to fall for it."

"Ye're no fool, lass; just trusting. Ye thought he'd be a decent guy, when he's nothing more than an arse." Anger bubbled up inside him, that James could make her second-guess herself, and that he'd treat her so poorly. "Ye said he's not capable of violence, and yet he's obviously capable of deception and going through yer computer files."

"I know. I just can't think of him as violent."

"Well, I can. He obviously cares for nothing but what will benefit him and him alone. And how did he get access to yer office? I can't imagine ye'd leave yer door unlocked."

"What does it matter?"

Annoyance crept into his voice. "It matters because I need to know exactly how far he'll go. If he stole yer keys and had copies made, then that's a wee bit different to finding yer door open—though not by much. If he went to those lengths for a bloody research paper, then just think what he'd do to get his hands on a priceless piece like the Hope."

"You're right." She closed her eyes, her brow furrowed with worry. "And the worst part is, if it was him snooping around, then he probably saw all the paintings we've pulled out and will know we're up to something."

"Then our only option is to find the necklace before James has a chance to act."

CHAPTER Seven

CAT IGNORED HER nerves as Iain introduced her to his brother, Malcolm. "It's a pleasure."

There were definite similarities in the men's looks. Both were tall and good-looking, with dark wavy hair, and those intelligent blue eyes. Yet Malcolm seemed to have a completely different air about him, as if he didn't have a care in the world when in the presence of anyone female.

"The pleasure's mine." He shook her hand with a curious smile and a glint in his eyes, his touch lingering a second longer than one would expect. "Iain's girlfriend? I hadn't realized."

Even though Malcolm lived in Edinburgh, they'd decided it'd be best to keep up the charade of being in a relationship, in case Malcolm spoke with anyone from town. Even if James figured out they weren't truly a couple, it'd still be best to keep up appearances, so others wouldn't start to suspect their true motivations.

"It's been a bit of a long-distance thing." Iain wrapped an arm around her shoulder, his eyes lingering on hers to reinforce their lie. "We'll not stay long, but I appreciate ye taking Da on such short notice."

Malcolm gave his father a smile and put a hand on the old man's shoulder. "Anytime. The two of us will find plenty to keep us entertained and busy. Won't get into too much trouble, will we, Da?"

Iain's smile turned stiff, though it was only for a second. "Can I speak to ye a moment?"

Without waiting for an answer Iain walked into another room, waited for Malcolm to join him, and then shut the door.

"Dinnae fash yerself, girl." Callum patted her arm, before taking a seat. "They've ne'er quite seen eye to eye, and Iain, being the oldest, has always taken it upon himself to care for everything and everyone."

She'd noticed. Cat still thought Iain was being a bit paranoid about James, especially going to the extent of having his father stay with his brother. Still, better safe than sorry. He was right about people going to extreme measures when there was fame and fortune to gain.

"Well, I hope I'll get to see you again before I leave Dunmuir. I've yet to hear any of your stories."

"Och well, Iain probably knows them better than I do at this point." He laughed, his blue eyes kind and keen. "And don't let his gruff exterior get to ye—he's a lamb underneath it all. But I think ye already knew that. He's used to getting his way, so don't go letting him push ye around. Put him in his place if ye see fit."

Before she could say anything, the door opened and the brothers joined them. The air in the room suddenly felt charged with tension. Iain turned to his father. "Like we discussed. And if you need anything at all, ye have my number."

"Aye, son. Take care."

"Will do, Da." Iain then turned a harsh gaze on his brother. "I'll be in touch."

They headed out the door and down the stairs, his walk brisk and his stride long.

She picked up her pace to keep up with him. "I don't suppose you want to tell me what that was about?"

"Ye supposed right. This isn't a real relationship, Cat."

"Luckily!"

They climbed into Iain's car, and before she'd even buckled up, he'd pulled out. "Bloody hell, Iain."

He pounded the steering wheel in frustration, gritting his teeth and taking a long breath. "Sorry."

"Look, I don't mean to be nosy, but if we're going to be stuck together for the foreseeable future, then maybe…"

"Maybe what? Maybe we can do each other's hair and confess all our secret crushes like a bunch of school girls? It's not happening, love." He flicked her a glance through narrowed eyes, his jaw tight and his entire body bristling with tension.

"Then I refuse to be on the receiving end of your wrath. I get being angry. But if you're not going to talk to me about whatever dragged your beautiful sunshiny mood out to play, then you need to vent elsewhere. I have no problem with you being upset, but if you're going to have a fit, then you better start talking."

Iain glared at her, his hands tight around the wheel. "Do ye not have any siblings that drive ye absolutely mad? Or are they all as perfect as you?"

"You're being a real jerk, Iain."

He said nothing for a long while, and Cat refused to speak to him. She knew families could be a pain, and whatever had gone down between Iain and his brother seemed to have really ticked him off. Still. She wasn't going to be the punching bag for his sour moods.

He swerved the car over to the side of the road and threw the gear into park, spinning in his seat to face her. "A jerk? Maybe I am. But guess what? Ye're stuck with me, just like I'm stuck with you. So deal with it."

"That's where you're wrong. I don't have to deal with it, Iain. I'll find the jewels without you. You can take your help and shove it up your Scottish arse."

She flung the door open, furious, and stepped out into the rain that always seemed to be falling, slamming the door behind her. He came after her, but she ignored him and kept moving down the road, refusing to acknowledge him. Tears stung her eyes as she wondered whether she'd just thrown out her one chance of finding the jewels. Yet she refused to back down.

He grabbed her hand, and she flinched, pain surging up her arm as her cut started to throb. "Shit! Sorry."

She pulled her hand away and kept walking, leaving him to try and catch up.

"Cat. Ye're getting drenched. Come back to the car."

When she continued to ignore him, he picked up his pace and cut her off, so he was now standing in her path. He gently grabbed her arms to keep her from escaping and was met with a glare.

"Let go of me, Iain. I'll find my own back to Dunmuir."

"And what then? Ye're staying with me. Remember?"

She laughed, ignoring the burn in her eyes. "You really think I'm still staying with you? Think again. I'm gone as soon as I grab my stuff and my car. And even that will be far too much time spent in your company."

His eyes narrowed in scrutiny, before his gaze softened. "Cat... I'm sorry."

He cupped her cheek, and before she could pull away, he kissed her, his lips on hers in a sweet and tender kiss. She resisted, but could only manage it for a moment.

Her head spun as their kiss deepened, her heart racing as he pulled her in close, her body molding to his, as she forgot about the other people walking by, forgot about the rain pouring down on them, and forgot about why she'd been mad at him.

When their kiss finally slowed, he still held her close, his eyes searching her face. "Can ye forgive me?"

She let out a weary sigh, fighting through the dizziness of that kiss. "Yes—but only if you stop being a jerk. I certainly don't need to know your life story and I'm not one to pry, but if whatever's going on with you is going to affect our working relationship, then I need to know about it. I told you about James, didn't I? Now it's your turn to spill the beans."

"Our working relationship?" His lips quirked into a smile as he leaned in to kiss her again—only to have her pull away.

"And that kiss? That never happened."

"Never happened, aye?" His smug grin and her racing heart had her pulling out of his arms and walking back to the car.

"No, it didn't. And whatever didn't happen is not going to happen again. You hear me?"

His eyes sparkled with amusement as they got into his car. "Aye, love. It ne'er happened and I swear I won't ne'er kiss ye again."

"Was that a double negative?" The only response she got was a laugh as he pulled out into traffic and headed towards home.

"Duncan?" Iain called out but the dog didn't come. "That's odd."

Cat could see Iain was worried. And then they heard a bark. "Down the hall. One of the rooms down there."

Iain opened the closed door, and the dog came barreling towards them in a full body wiggle. "Did ye get yerself trapped? Come on then. It's been a long day. Go on out."

Iain let Duncan out, but the dog only took a few minutes before running back in.

"I think he missed you."

"Something's not quite right. He seems panicked." Iain knelt down and grabbed the dog, murmuring to him to try and calm him down. "Are ye alright, pup? What happened?"

"It's probably because he got locked in the room."

"Aye, but that's unusual in and of itself. The doors will catch a draft from time to time and slam shut, but it doesn't happen that often, and not when all the windows are closed." Iain dug into his pocket. "Take my keys. I want ye to wait for me in my car."

"You think someone broke in?" She felt the surge of adrenaline as her heart started to pound. "The paintings and letters."

She raced forward, but he grabbed her arm, preventing her moving past him. "If ye're not going to listen to me, then we'll go together. Stay behind me, and if I tell ye to go, ye're to run to my car and lock the doors."

He grabbed the shotgun from the closet, checked the ammunition and then moved forward towards the library, poking his head in the other rooms as they went past.

Cat saw the paintings, but couldn't find the rest. "The letters and journals are gone."

Iain stood by his desk, fumbling with a key. "I locked them away before leaving this morning. They're still here."

Cat let out a huge sigh of relief. "Bloody hell. I nearly had a heart attack."

Iain looked around the room, pulling back the curtains, before heading for the hall. "Stay here with Duncan. I'm going to check out the rest of the house. Make sure to lock the door behind me."

She wanted to tell Iain he was being paranoid again, but she remembered the footsteps on the patio last night, and knew he was right to be cautious. While she waited, she took the time to go through their items to make sure nothing had gone missing. If someone had riffled through things, they'd done a decent enough job of leaving them undisturbed—just like James had done with her laptop and computer.

If it was him—and in all likelihood, it was—Iain would have a hard time keeping her from murdering the lying, sneaky ass. She still couldn't believe she'd been stupid enough to fall for James.

As for Iain and that kiss? What the hell had she been thinking? She could *not* let herself get caught in that trap, and she most definitely had to stop replaying their kiss over and over in her mind. It was a one-off, and it had to stay that way. She had to focus on what was important, and that was finding the Highlander's Hope—not some steamy entanglement with a cantankerous laird.

The knock on the library door was followed by Iain's voice and Duncan trotting across the room. Cat let Iain in, but already knew he had bad news if the look on his face was anything to go by.

"There's a broken pane in the room we found Duncan in, and a grease stain on the rug, in addition to an unlocked door they likely used to leave."

"That makes sense then. They could keep Duncan distracted with food, giving them time to close the door behind them, and then leave using a different exit."

"Did ye have a closer look to make sure things didn't go missing?"

"I don't think he took anything, but there's a good chance he got photos of the paintings and may have found my notes, though they were tucked away in my work bag." She shook her head. "I swear, if I see James again…"

"If ye see him, ye're to pretend nothing happened. It'll only reinforce that ye're looking for something of value." He took her hand and pulled her in close, nuzzling her cheek, as she tried not to turn towards his lips, her heart racing to have him so near. "For now, we're going to keep pretending to be a couple, without a care in the world. I doubt he knows what we're looking for, and we might still be able to get away with him thinking the paintings and your notes were nothing more than your curiosity about my clan."

"Are you sure this isn't just an excuse to kiss me again?" Her eyebrow perked in question, but really, her cool demeanor was nothing more than a façade to cover up the inner voice telling her she'd lost her mind.

He leaned in with a smile, tucking a stray curl behind her ear. "Again? I don't recall any kiss, my dear. Nor will I recall this…"

With an arm around her waist, he brushed his lips against hers in a whisper, before trailing kisses down the curve of her neck and over to her ear, sending a shiver of need through to her very core. She leaned against him as he kissed her full on the lips, her hands fisting his shirt as she lost herself in him, his hard body pressed against hers.

When she finally managed to undo their lip-lock, she was short of breath and her body felt like it was on fire. Good thing he was still holding onto her too, since her legs felt like taffy on a hot summer day.

"Ye're blushing, love."

"That didn't happen either."

"Of course not."

"What are we going to do about James?" Turning the conversation back to the true matter at hand seemed to be her safest bet. As soon as she felt stable on her feet, she slipped out of his arms, cursing herself for being weak again.

She reminded herself that she was dealing with a man who changed his women more frequently than it rained in Scotland. Though she had no problem with the occasional fling or one night stand, she could see herself ending up with a broken heart if she wasn't careful. Somehow he kept managing to get past her defenses.

"I think paying him a friendly visit might help him rethink any further mischief. We'll play up that we think he's a jealous ex, but still won't mention the research or the paintings. Might help to reinforce the idea that we're just a couple." He brushed her cheek, his touch lingering, slipping into his role of boyfriend far too easily. "That'll have to wait until tomorrow though, since we're now going to find us those jewels. What do ye say?"

"Let's get started then." She was relieved to get back to work and put a bit of space between them. "Should we go through the paintings or the journals first?"

"The paintings, since they'll be quicker. That way we can either check them off the list or look into them further." Iain ran a hand through his hair as he looked around at the paintings. "Maybe if we line them up?"

She started propping them against the bookshelves, trying her best to sort them by time period. Most of them appeared to be of the MacCraigh home and land, and its inhabitants. Some of the scenery even made more than one appearance.

Cat pulled out her cell phone. "Maybe we should take a picture of each? They could have easily been stolen today, and then we wouldn't have them for reference."

"Aye. It's a good idea. Some sort of security wouldn't go amiss, either."

While she took a snap of each painting, including close-ups, he squatted down in front of them to get a better look. Done with the photos, she joined him in front of Nessa's portrait.

"Anything?"

Iain tilted his head to the side as if trying to see something from a different angle.

"Right there." He pointed to an area around her neck and chest, which had been modestly covered with ruffled lace. "Is it just me, or does it look like there's just a ghost of a necklace underneath that sheer fabric?"

Cat leaned in for a closer look, and then pulled away to see if it could be better seen from a distance. "I suppose there could be something there under the folds, but it might also be the shading. It's hard to tell."

"Aye. It's a pity it's not more definitive."

She looked at the paintings again. "I noticed that in a few of these, the same bit of landscape seems to keep showing up. You'd think that with all the surrounding lands, they might paint something other than the same rocky outcrop. Or does it have some special clan significance?"

"This one here?" He pointed to the scenery that could be seen out the window of the portrait. "No. No significance at all. But ye know what *is* interesting? It's not accurate. This part here is correct. It's as ye'd see it from the window in the sitting room. But ye see this wall of stone here? I recognize it. And I can tell ye, there's no way ye'd be able to see if from the house."

She got a jolt of excitement. "Do you think that could be it then?"

He shrugged with a smile. "We've still got a few hours of daylight, if ye feel like a bit of a hike."

"Give me a sec, and I'll get changed." With a huge smile and an adrenaline high pounding through her veins, she trotted off to the room she was staying in.

And swallowed her scream.

CHAPTER
Eight

C AT'S STIFLED CRY had Iain running up the stairs, taking them two and three at a time. He caught her just as she burst out of her room, quickly taking her in to make sure she wasn't hurt. "What's happened? Are ye all right?"

She nodded, but had yet to speak. When she finally did, it was through a jaw clenched tight with anger. "He was here. James."

He stepped past her and into the guest room, immediately taking in the scene. A dead dove lay in the middle of her bed, staining the covers with its blood, the curtains billowing in front of an open window.

"I'm sorry I didn't check yer room. I hadn't wanted to invade yer privacy. And ye think this is also James?"

Cat nodded. "He used to call me his little dove. It could be a coincidence, but since we already think he broke in, I doubt the bird's an accident."

"Aye, I agree. I'm starting to think he'll stop at nothing to get what he wants. Breaking into my home and threatening my guest? I'll not stand for it." He'd be damned if he was going to let it happen again. "He'll not get away with this, Cat."

"Damn right. If he thinks this is going to scare me off, then he's in for a rude awakening. Are you still up for that hike?"

He loved her determination, but worried it was affecting her more than she was letting on. Still, the sooner they found the necklace, the better. "Ye can move into the room across the hall. If ye want to grab yer things, I'll clean this up."

Her hand was gentle as she brushed his arm, her gaze finding his. "Thank you."

She left his side to gather her things, but he could still feel her touch lingering on his skin. What the hell was he doing? He cursed himself for growing attached to her. Their ruse had done more than get the village talking—it'd shown him just what it would be like to have her at his side.

Under normal circumstances, he'd keep it casual—not that he'd have given her a second look before all this began. The parade of models he'd dated were more his style, and yet... he'd never been so annoyed, interested, or turned on.

Well, if nothing else, they'd help each other find the jewels, and keep each other entertained in the process. She was nothing more than a fleeting interest fueled by the mystery and excitement of a treasure hunt.

He grabbed the covers and sheets off the bed, the bird bundled within, and took them out to the trash, after a passing thought that he should call the police. There'd be little chance of them doing anything more than filing a report, so he quickly dismissed it. The last thing he needed was his name in the tabloids, and he knew if they caught wind of it, they'd somehow manage to spin it into a maelstrom of a story—not to mention they'd latch onto Cat as his latest fling. He could only imagine her reaction to *that*.

By the time he got on his hiking boots and grabbed his jacket, Cat was coming down the stairs in a warm sweater and jeans that hugged every curve on a body one wouldn't expect on a historian. "Ready?"

She grabbed her jacket from the coat rack and put it on, flicking her hair free from under her collar. She'd been wearing it down since he kept yanking out her hair clip every chance he got, under the guise that she shouldn't look like she was working if they were pretending she was on a romantic getaway. Truth was he hated to see her trying to tame her locks, when those curls clearly wanted to bounce free.

"Ready." She gave him a smile, but it seemed forced.

"Are ye sure ye're doing all right? We can leave it for tomorrow, if ye're not up for it. It is rather late for a hike." He was worried about her. The implied threat of the dead bird would be enough to have most abandoning the project and bolting from town. Yet here she stood ready to soldier on, as if she hadn't a care in the world.

"You worry too much, Iain MacCraigh. Now, come on. I'll be damned if I'm going to let James find the necklace first."

The rain settled into a fine mist. Being born and bred a highlander, the weather didn't tend to bother him much, yet he wasn't alone on their adventure, and suspected Cat would be frozen to the bone by the time they made it back.

He turned to conversation to distract her from the cold, while guiding her through the woods. "So what made ye decide to study Scottish history? Seems like an odd choice for an American."

"It was my Gran. She grew up not far from here. When I was little, she would tell me all sorts of stories about Prince Charlie's Jacobites, and the clans." Her eyes sparkled as she recalled her childhood. "There weren't many programs in the States, so when I got accepted to Cambridge, I jumped at the chance. Would have liked to go to Edinburgh, but Cambridge gave me a full scholarship."

"Hard to do better than Cambridge. And yer Gran sounds like my own Grannie—and Mrs. Wallace, whom ye've yet to meet. I think every Scot is raised on the stories of old." When they got to a craggy outcropping, he reached back and took her hand to help her over the uneven terrain and to be there if she lost her footing. "We're nearly there."

The path they were on was narrow and not clearly visible unless you knew where to look. He led her up a steep incline, the rock face he was looking for just up ahead. "Careful. It's a long tumble to the bottom of the hill."

When she looked over her shoulder, her grip on his hand tightened. "Yeah... you aren't kidding."

He pulled her closer to him and onto surer ground, before leading her through some trees. "There it is."

A large chunk of pink granite jutted out from the cliff side at an odd angle. Flecks of dark grey interspersed through the rose-colored stone, along with crystalline segments that caught the light of the sun, now low on the horizon. Surrounding the granite was a dark grey sandy-textured stone, formed in such a way as to shape the granite into something resembling a heart if viewed from the right angle.

"It's just like in the painting—except there's no way in hell you'd see this rock face from any window at your home."

"Yet if ye didn't know the area well, ye might not notice that it didn't belong." He took her by the shoulders and gently shifted her to the side. "Do ye see it now?"

She looked up at him with a smile. "It's a heart, right?"

"Aye, it goes by several names, but I've always known it as the Bleeding Heart. It was probably called that because of the way the dark grey stone sort of cuts the heart in half. However, the real question is, how does this lead us to the necklace?" Iain started to search around for any rifts in the rock where someone might be able to stash something, but turned up empty.

"Could it be buried here?" She gave him a crooked grin, her hair flying in the wind.

"I suppose so, though without a metal detector or tearing up half the hill, I'm not sure how we'd find it, short of it being buried right here."

"I don't suppose you have a metal detector?" Her lips quirked into a smile.

"No, love. I usually make my money rather than go digging for it. Sorry to disappoint. And it's not like we know for sure that this is actually a clue." He couldn't recall any stories about the stone itself, and the other names had long escaped his memory. "When we get back, I'll call my father. There's a good chance he might know some of the local lore."

"It could also be that it's only part of a clue. It might be that there are several pieces that work together. It would be another way to safeguard the necklace from falling into the wrong hands."

"That makes sense. Why don't we head back then and take a look at the other paintings? It'll be dark before long, and I'd rather not get us stranded out here for the night." Iain was familiar enough with the woods around his home, but he was without any light source, and it'd be too easy for Cat to misstep and hurt herself. She didn't exactly have a great track record around him.

Not wanting her to slip on the way down, Iain took her hand. "Careful. And if ye need me to slow down, just say so."

As steep as the path was, they both ended up slipping and sliding their way down the hill, holding each other up half the time. By the time they finally made it back, they were wet, cold, and dark had fallen.

"Go get changed into something dry, while I get us some tea." Even Iain was cold to the bone, though he didn't regret going out. It felt like they were one step closer to finding the jewels, though he was also two steps closer to wanting Cat. Now that they'd actually gotten started with the research, he thought they worked rather well together.

"Forget about the tea for a few minutes. You'll catch your death if you don't get out of those clothes."

"I could think of other ways to get warm, if ye're interested." Did those words really just come out of his mouth?

Her brows perked up, and a stern yet amused look danced in her eyes. "You didn't just say that."

The way her lips curled into a lazy smile made him want to show her exactly what he had in mind. Why he was having such a hard time staying away from her was beyond him.

"Say what? I don't seem to recall." Yet his arm wrapped around her waist and pulled her close.

The furious blush that covered her cheeks only made him want her more—and that was a problem. He was *not* good at hanging around the morning after, and she was definitely the type who couldn't do casual. It'd be stupid to ruin their working relationship when there was so much at stake, and yet…

He leaned in to kiss her and was met with a hand on his chest. "This is a bad idea."

"It is." His next attempt fared no better. "So then why can't I help myself?"

"Because you've obviously had every woman you've ever been interested in fall into bed with you." She scoffed out a laugh at him. "You're good looking, rich, and a land-owning laird with his own little castle. I doubt many have refused you."

He should be offended rather than amused and wanting her even more. "Are ye sure it's not my irresistible charms?"

"Truth is, I don't know how I've managed to keep my clothes on around you." She looked at him with exaggerated doe-eyes, blinking her lashes at him. "My heart just pitter-patters every time you're near, and my clothes want to fall to the floor."

He threw his hands up in mock surrender, finally letting her go. "All right then. I give up. I know when I've been beaten."

She just shrugged, her eyes sparkling with mischief. "Night's not over yet, *m'laird.*"

"Did ye really just say that?"

Though her face was a mask, her eyes were filled with humor. "Say what? I don't seem to recall."

"Right here." Iain pointed to a painting of his family home, hillsides and loch sprawling just beyond. "The loch is out of place. Not by much, mind ye, but enough."

"I think you've solved the key that'll lead us to the necklace. Misplaced landmarks—it'd be another layer of protection, right? Only someone familiar with the area would be able to crack the code." She grabbed his arm in excitement. "We may actually find it, Iain."

"Let me call my father. He may have information on the landmarks that could shed a bit more light." He pulled out his cell and explained what he needed.

His father was happy to oblige, and told him all that he remembered, Iain's excitement growing as he listened to the lore. Thanking his father, he hung up and turned to Cat who was anxiously waiting.

"The Bleeding Heart used to go by a different name a good century or so ago, and was known as the Smuggler's Heart. And the loch? It was also known to be part of a smuggler's route. I hadn't realized, but according to my father, we had a few smugglers in the family who managed to do quite well for themselves."

"Smugglers and lairds, huh?" She pulled her hair back, gave it a quick twist and pinned it back with a silver clip, making him want to curse.

"Aye. Must be how they were able to hold onto their position of power through the harder times after the war. Likely bribed their way past any seizures of land." He tugged at one of the stray curls that didn't make it into the clip, resisting the urge to tug her hair free. "And the best part? There were rumors of secret tunnels hidden on our land."

She nearly vibrated with excitement, and her smile was contagious. "Is there any way to find out where they might be?"

"I don't know, love. But we'll figure something out." He got up and grabbed her hand, pulling her to her feet, so they stood together facing each other, their bodies brushing. "Dinner. I'm starving, and if I don't eat, I'm liable to find something else to distract me from my hunger."

"Is that so?"

"Aye, it is." He reached over and pulled the clip from her hair, running his fingers through it to free her curls. "How many of these cursed hair things do you have, anyway? I swear, I've stolen a half dozen, yet they keep coming back."

"Do you think this is a wise idea?" She glanced away for just a second, uncertainty worrying that pretty face of hers.

"Dinner? Usually it is, though I guess we could be unconventional and opt for a very late—or early, depending on how you look at it—breakfast." Iain knew it wasn't what she was referring to, but he certainly wasn't in any mood to discuss their casual flirtations and turn them into something serious. "Come on, Cat. It's just dinner."

"It's not dinner I'm concerned with." She sighed, gave her head a quick shake, and then looked at him with a smile, as if her concerns had evaporated. "You're right. I'm starving. Dinner it is."

"We'll head into town, if that's all right. I want to make sure we keep up appearances, so people don't think we're up to anything more than just enjoying each other."

"Enjoying each other, huh? Nice choice of words there."

Unable to resist, he nuzzled her, his heart thudding against his chest. "I do try."

"I noticed." She turned towards him, her lips only a whisper away.

"I can't imagine people will suspect we're not a couple." He brushed his lips against hers, and then nipped at them.

She shifted away, though only far enough to look him in the eyes. "Except for James. If he broke in here, then he knows we're looking at the paintings."

Iain shrugged and wrapped his arm around her waist. "They're just paintings, and they could easily have been in the library for storage. It's not like he found the letters and journals. We just need to make sure he has no doubts about why ye're here. Do ye think ye're up for a dinner and a stroll through town on a Saturday night?"

She leaned against him, their cheeks touching as she spoke, her lips at his ear. "I'll admit, I'm finding it easier to play my role as of late."

His chest tightened with need, and he knew if he didn't pull away, he'd try taking her then and there on the library sofa. Better if they made good use of the sexual tension between them to make their ruse more convincing—though he was starting to wonder just how much of a ruse it actually was.

How he found the strength to pull away from her, he didn't know. "We should go. But we need not stay out long. I promise to have ye back to yer paintings and journals in no time at all."

Her eyes narrowed for a moment, as if she was trying to decipher him. In the end, she gave him a smile and threw on her jacket. "I'll hold you to that, then."

Yet during the drive into town, he could feel her gaze on him. "What's wrong?"

"Nothing. Just wondering."

"Wondering what?" By the gods, he doubted it was anything good.

"Why you're still single."

"Me? Too busy with work. I haven't the time or desire to pursue anything serious." His rote answer came tumbling out by habit before he'd given it much thought—and now he regretted it. He liked Cat more than he was willing to admit, and maybe more so because his interest in her had been completely unexpected, especially given how they started. "Not that I'd let the right lass pass me by."

Her laugh made him smile. "Good answer, MacCraigh."

"Aye, I thought so myself." By the gods, the woman kept him on his toes at least. He didn't think he'd ever find himself bored in her company—an all too frequent occurrence with most of the women he dated.

He parked, and then shifted in his seat to face her. "Are ye ready then? The more people who see us together the easier it'll be to pass us off as a happy couple in love."

"I just want James to go away. I hate knowing he's snooping around. It puts me on edge." Her smile faded, leaving Iain all the more furious that James had such a negative effect on her.

"Cat, I know we've not known each other long, but I swear I'll do all I can to protect ye from that bastard." The possessiveness he felt over her was unlike anything he'd felt before, and Iain realized it was because it didn't come from a place of control or jealousy, but rather a place where he needed to do right by her and keep her safe.

"I appreciate it." Her eyes sparkled in the dark of night, caught by the street lights, as her hand cupped his cheek and her thumb brushed his lips, before she kissed him sweetly. "I'm ready if you are?"

"Aye, love." Never had he been more ready, though he knew it was for far more than a meal and stroll through town. As if to reinforce what they were doing and to keep his mind from being sidetracked, he said, "Dinner."

With her tucked by his side, they headed towards the pub, knowing it'd be the busiest place in town. They grabbed a seat at a booth, but before they'd even gotten their food, Angus slid into the spot next to Iain, a shit-eating grin on his face.

Ignoring Iain, Angus turned his charms and attention on Cat. "I hope ye don't mind my joining ye. It's just that Iain so rarely brings around his dates, and when he does, they seldom have much of interest to say."

"And what makes you think I'm any different?" Her eyes sparked alight, a teasing smile dancing on those full kissable lips.

"Even a blind man could see ye've got plenty to say, and it'd be nothing but interesting. Is that not right, Iain?" Angus's smiling face turned towards him, making Iain want to curse.

"Aye, though I don't know what has ye so interested in my love life, when ye should be concerned about yer own. Can't remember the last time ye brought around a lass."

Angus turned back to Cat, ignoring Iain. "So will ye be staying with us long? Iain will have to show ye the standing stones. They're not far from here."

"I'm here for at least another week or two, though I'll have to return to Cambridge before long." Cat reached out and took Iain's hand with a smile that lit up her face. "We haven't gotten to the stones yet, but I've enjoyed myself thoroughly. I'll be sorry to go when the time comes."

Iain could see his friend was starting to wonder if he'd been mistaken about them not being a couple. He hated keeping the truth from him, but telling Angus about the jewels would only complicate matters. He'd tell him everything once it was over with.

Cat squeezed his hand, her smile fading. Iain followed her gaze, already knowing whom he'd find. Anger rose within him like a loosened beast. "Move, Angus."

His friend looked at him in question, but got to his feet, as Cat held onto his hand, her grip tightening.

"Iain, it's not worth it."

But already he was gone, riding a wave of fury.

CHAPTER
Nine

C AT COULDN'T GET to Iain fast enough to stop him. Blood was
pouring from James's nose, and Iain was getting ready to throw
another punch, when Angus grabbed hold of him and wrestled
him away.

"I'll fucking kill ye if ye threaten Cat again. Do ye hear me? I'll tear
ye limb from limb." Iain still struggled to get free, but Angus was strong
enough to keep hold of him.

Angus turned Iain away from James, waiting for him to stop struggling.
"I'm going to let ye go now, aye? Don't make me regret it."

Iain shrugged free as Angus let him go, and Cat rushed to his side.
"Are you ok?"

Iain nodded while glaring at James, who didn't have enough sense to
stay away.

"I'm calling the authorities. You can't get away with this." James was furious, his nose yet to stop bleeding.

"Go ahead. Call. Then maybe while we're at it, ye can explain to them how ye broke into my home and threatened my girlfriend."

Angus's eyes narrowed in question as he took a step closer to James. "Is it true? Cause I like Cat, and if I find out ye're mistreating her in any way, I won't be happy. Might have to let my friend have another go at ye. Are we clear?"

Picking on the only one there smaller than him, James turned his attention on her. "I'll be sure you pay for this. This isn't over, Cat."

"I think it is. And if you bother me again, I'll make sure your nose never sets properly."

Cat watched James leave but knew the matter was far from over. He was prideful, and his ego had been wounded in a very public way.

Iain pulled her into his arms protectively. "Are ye all right?"

She looked up at him, feeling emotional now that the adrenaline was starting to wear off. "Me? You're the one who's probably busted half your fingers."

He brushed her cheek, and kissed her. "And I'll do it again if he even looks at ye the wrong way. I won't have him threatening ye, Cat."

Angus looked at the two of them, and then sat down, letting her and Iain slide in across from him. The pub had gone quiet during the fight, and was now returning to normal.

Angus shook his head. "Let me see yer hand. Cat's probably right. I've ne'er seen ye hit anyone so hard. Hand."

Iain's knuckles were scraped and already swelling. Angus carefully worked his way down each finger, his lips pursed in annoyance. "So are ye going to tell me what the hell is going on around here? I know something's up. I'm not an idiot, Iain."

"No, ye're the most brilliant man I know. And if there was something going on and I could tell ye, I would."

"But ye can't tell me." Angus looked from Iain to Cat. "Well, I'm here if ye need me. Ye lucked out on that hand. Ye didn't break anything, though ye still may have a fracture. I'd tell ye to ice it and have it checked, but I know ye won't."

"I appreciate it. All of it."

Angus slipped out of his seat and got ready to go. "Take care of him, Cat. And you—call me if ye need me, Iain. For anything."

"Aye, man." Iain watched his friend go, before turning back to Cat. "I hate not telling him, but I'll not put him in harm's way."

"About James… you shouldn't have gone after him, Iain. He's got a nasty streak and won't think twice about retaliating. This could easily get out of control."

"It got out of control when he stole yer research the first time around. As for now? He's the one who started this. And I'll be damned if I'm just going to stand by and let him threaten ye and invade my home."

He looked at her with such intensity, it all but took her breath away. And when he kissed her, with the adrenaline from the fight spurring them on, it was like the world had fallen away from beneath her feet. She lost herself in him, feeling herself tumble.

She knew she should just take things as they come, whether it turned out to be nothing more than a fun romp or something more. And yet… it felt like her heart was on the line. "Iain… what are we doing?"

He kissed her nose. "Ye can't control this sort of thing, Cat. Ye just need to let it go where it will."

Maybe he was right. But could she really take such a risk? It hadn't turned out so well in the past. And this time? She could already tell that if she gave into the feelings she'd been trying to ignore, she'd fall hard.

"Is that what you normally do, MacCraigh? Just let things happen as they will?"

He smiled shyly. "No, love. But I think I might give it a try this time around."

After dinner, they made their way back to Iain's and settled in the library once more. Cat poured over the journals, while Iain continued to analyze the paintings. Most of the writings were unrelated to what they were looking for, and more about the crops and weather, along with details of marriages and births.

"I'm not finding too much here. How about you?" Cat got up and stretched before heading over to Iain, who also stood and proceeded to yawn.

"I need a cup of tea."

"You realize it's close to midnight, right?" She was normally in bed and sound asleep by ten.

"Do ye need to be somewhere at the crack of dawn? I was thinking we might sleep in."

The look in his eyes and the way he'd said *'we'* had her heart tripping over itself. It sounded far too much like he expected them to be waking up together—as in tangled-limbs-and-naked-the-morning-after together.

"Ye're blushing." He took a step closer, and her additional step back had her falling over a bronze dog statue, just as he caught her in his arms and pulled her close. "Careful there, love. I wouldn't want ye hurting yerself."

"Could you please stop looking at me like that?"

"Like what?" His eyebrow quirked up in amusement.

Her breath caught in her throat, and her voice sounded thin, like she couldn't quite get enough air into her lungs to speak. "It's like you're a cat that's caught a mouse and you're going to play with your new toy until you're ready to devour it."

"That sounds about right."

Cat stammered like an idiot, not knowing what to say.

"I'm kidding, Cat."

Yet he still hadn't let her go. "Are you really?"

"No, I'm not."

She couldn't even begin to decipher what that meant with the double negatives, and the fact that the nearness of him had fried her brain. And he still had *that look*, though it was now laced with humor.

"Why do I put ye on edge?"

"I don't know." She bit her lip. "I'm no good at this sort of thing, Iain."

"At flirting?" He nuzzled against her cheek, and then nibbled at her ear, sending a shiver of need pulsing through her. "I like that I make you a little bit nervous."

"I've noticed." She tried to resist him, but found it futile, her body pressed against his as he kissed her.

When he finally pulled away, she found herself lightheaded, desperately holding onto him to keep from melting to the floor.

"You need to stop doing that." Either that or he had to *not* stop. One or the other.

"Do I?" He kissed her again, and she was more than happy to return his attentions. His words were but a husky whisper. "I'll admit, I'd be disappointed if I could no longer kiss ye."

"Would you really? Or is that what you tell all the girls?"

She'd been half-joking when she said it, but he pulled away, his eyes locked on hers, his mood serious.

"Cat…" He brushed a stray curl from her face, his touch lingering, as if he hadn't quite wanted to let her go. "I'll admit I likely deserve whatever it is ye think of me with regards to women, but I'm telling ye now, this is different. How exactly? I don't know, if I'm being honest, but it *is* different."

She wrapped her arms around her waist, feeling unsure of herself and her feelings for him. But if he was being honest with her, then she should probably return the favor. "It's been different for me too—and I think that's why I'm feeling skittish. I really like you, Iain."

"And I you—a hell of a lot more than I'd ever expected to." He pulled her close and kissed the top of her head. After lingering a moment more, he stepped back as if to give her the space she still needed. "How about that tea?"

"Sounds perfect."

"I can't believe it's such a gorgeous day." The morning had arrived with clear blue skies and the temperatures feeling more like early September rather than late October. It left Cat feeling like anything was possible.

"The loch's not much farther. Ye holding up all right?"

Iain glanced her way, and she thought he looked far too handsome and rugged. He hadn't bothered to shave, and his loose curls kept catching the wind, his dark locks making his blue eyes stand out in contrast. She had been so mistaken about him in the beginning. The last thing she'd expected was to find someone who was funny and sweet, considerate and caring—even if he could be brash and impulsive at times.

"I'm thoroughly enjoying myself." Busy as she was, she seldom got the chance to go on hikes. "So, you think the tunnels are close by?"

"Aye. We're not far from the sea, and there are naturally formed caves and tunnels throughout the area. Since we know there were smugglers in my clan, it's likely they had once used them to move around undetected and stash their goods. Just a matter of finding them. My father mentioned a few areas we should check."

"I really like your father."

"Aye, he's a good man. And so ye know, he likes you too." He tilted his head to look at her, amusement in his eyes.

"What? I'm likable."

Iain barked out a laugh. "I'll have ye know that though he's always been polite and charming to the few dates I've actually brought home and has wanted me to be happy, I don't think he's e'er been terribly impressed."

"And am I one of your dates then?" Not that she needed to put a label on what they were doing, but she did like a neat and ordered world.

He shrugged. "No. I wouldn't say that."

She felt her back go up and her pace quicken. At least he was being honest. "Well, I appreciate your honesty."

He grabbed her arm and pulled her to a stop, turning her towards him so she was forced to look at him. Amusement quirked at his lips before he finally burst out a laugh. "Cat…"

"What?" Frustrated with him laughing at her, she glared at him. "I'm glad I can still entertain you."

"For such a smart girl, ye certainly can be a fool." When she turned to walk away, he pulled her into his arms. "Cat, I'm not lumping ye in with *my dates* because I've ne'er been remotely interested in them past dinner and the morning after. This is… new to me. And our pretending to be a couple? I don't want to pretend anymore."

"Oh." Bloody hell. Was she blushing again? She squeezed her eyes shut to try and decipher what he'd just said, since it felt like her brain was wading through molasses. Did he mean he didn't want to bother with the ruse anymore since James was likely onto them? Or was it that he didn't want to pretend, because he did indeed want to be with her?

Iain didn't give her the chance to think about it for long. He tilted her chin up and kissed her, kissed her like they were the only two people in the world, kissed her as if they might cease to exist if he stopped. She was breathless and dizzy by the time he finally stopped, though he still held her close.

"Are ye all right then—with not pretending? I want this to be real, Cat." He searched her face as if looking for an answer.

She tried to think about it logically, but in the end, the fluttering of her stomach and the racing of her heart overruled her brain. "I think I'd like that."

Cat kept telling herself that Iain was twice her size, and had managed to squeeze through the tiny opening in the hill side with little finagling. She would *not* get stuck. Taking a deep breath, she tried to ignore the feeling of being squeezed to death, and with Iain's helping hand, got through to the other side.

Cat looked around the cave, grateful Iain had brought along flashlights. "It's bigger than I expected."

"What every guy loves to hear."

She laughed at that one. The little light that made it in from the opening died only feet away. It was damp and smelled of the earth, and Cat wondered just how many spider webs she'd already walked through. It made her shudder.

"I don't think anyone's been here in decades—at least. The entrance is fairly well hidden from view, and unless ye knew where to look, it's unlikely anyone would find it. Not to mention, this is private property. People still hike through from time to time, but we're rather out of the way for most folks." He walked towards the darkness, shining his light around. "Looks like it continues."

Steeling herself to keep any newfound claustrophobia at bay, Cat followed Iain, grateful that the tunnel seemed to be getting both wider and taller. The tunnel continued relatively straight, with only a few bends, but before long, they stumbled onto a fork.

Iain pulled off his pack and dug around for a spool of twine. "I don't want to be the one responsible for getting us lost in these caves."

"Well, aren't you the boy scout. And let me just say, it's greatly appreciated, especially since," she pulled out her phone and checked the bars, "there is *no* reception in here."

"Do ye think I'd let us get lost?" Humor laced his voice as he looked at her in question.

"I think you'd do your best to keep that from happening."

"Good answer, Doctor." He gave her a quick kiss that made her stomach flutter and then looked around for a place to secure the twine, settling on a rock. "It's not ideal, but it'll have to do."

They picked a tunnel and followed it for another fifteen minutes before it ended to form a large room.

"Look." Iain pointed at rusty metal rings bolted into the rock wall. "They'd likely be used for holding torches."

"Seems like this area may have been used to store smuggled goods. Weapons too, during the Jacobite uprising." Excitement bubbled in her chest, and though Cat told herself they were still a long way off from finding the jewels, she couldn't help but feel they were one step closer.

Iain chewed his bottom lip, clearly deep in thought.

"What is it?"

"The entrance." Iain gave it some more thought. "It's rather narrow. I'm just wondering if there's another way in. One more suited to smuggling goods in and out of here."

She grabbed his hand, raring to go. "The other tunnel."

"Aye. That could be it."

CHAPTER Ten

THERE WERE FAR more twists and turns to the next tunnel they took. The air quality started to change, losing the stale and moldy scent. They had to be close to the mouth of the cave for the air to be as fresh as it was. The light then changed as they came around another corner, the darkness not quite as oppressive. "There. It should be just up ahead."

The end of the tunnel appeared, though the entrance was blocked by dense shrubbery. He flashed his light around to see if there were any clues, but there was nothing.

He turned to Cat. "We're one step closer, and there's still the last tunnel to explore, though that might have to wait. It's a pity there wasn't anything more conclusive in this one, but it's a start."

"Definitely. We can head back to the paintings and journals, and see if there's anything more. We'll find it, Iain."

He hoped she was right. He still needed the necklace as something to leverage for funds, if he had any hope of getting his family out from under his brother's troubles. The current market for high-end real estate was nonexistent, and with the economy on shaky ground, he couldn't even use the manor as collateral. All his other funds were tied up in business ventures and would be impossible to wrangle free.

Shaking himself free of his thoughts, he gave Cat a quick kiss, happy he could now do so without second-guessing himself. "Come, then. Let's see where we've ended up."

Iain squeezed past the branches and then held them aside for Cat to exit. He squinted against the light, waiting for his vision to return to normal. When he could finally keep his eyes open, he looked around.

"This way." He led her through the dense trees and shrubs before finding the path he was looking for. "Right there."

No more than a hundred yards away was the Bleeding Heart stone. It was one more connection.

Cat squeezed his hand, her face beaming with excitement. "We're on the right path, Iain."

He tucked a stray curl behind her ear, resisting the urge to kiss her again. "Aye, that we are."

By the time they made it home, the weather had started to turn, the sun streaking down from behind billowy clouds. He was looking forward to getting back to the paintings—and Cat. They worked well together, and he hoped it'd just be the start of it all.

His only worry stemmed from the uncertainty of how she'd react to him leveraging the jewels as collateral until he could liquidate his assets— if and when they found them. It's not like he was selling them—he could never bring himself to do that. But he still didn't think she'd be happy about him putting them temporarily on the line, even if it was to save his family's estate and his brother's arse.

As they came around to the front of the house, Iain bit back a curse. Speak of the devil. "My brother's here."

When she looked over at him, there were lines of worry marring her smooth skin. "There's nothing wrong with your father, is there?"

"I doubt that's the reason he's here. He likely wants something." Already, he'd said too much. The last thing he wanted was to drag Cat into his problems, especially this early in a relationship. The poor girl would go running for the hills if she knew. "It'll be fine. Don't go worrying yerself."

"If you need someone to talk to... I know we don't know each other that well, but I'm here if you need me."

He cupped her cheek, his fingers twined in her hair. "I know it hasn't been long, Cat, but I feel close to ye. I don't know if it's because of the intensity of our situation or if it's because ye're so different to anyone I've e'er known, but don't let some calendar tell ye how to feel. I appreciate ye being here for me. Truly."

Once he was sure she was all right, they went in as he steeled himself and his temper. They found him in the sitting room. "Malcolm, I hadn't expected ye. Is Da all right?"

"Aye, he's fine. No worries." Malcolm turned to Cat, all smiles and charm, making Iain grit his teeth. "Nice to see ye again, Cat."

Before Cat had a chance to greet his brother, Iain put a stop to all the niceties. "Ye'll excuse me for being blunt, but why are ye here?"

Iain wasn't in the mood for his brother's nonsense. He'd dealt it with it all his life and Malcolm had yet to learn from his mistakes. This latest mess had pushed Iain over the edge though. To put everything at risk— and drag their father into it, no less—was unforgiveable.

"I overheard yer conversation with Da." Malcolm looked smug, and it did nothing but annoy Iain. "About the Bleeding Heart and the loch."

"What about it? We're going for a hike, and Cat was curious about where the Heart got its name." The last thing he needed was his brother snooping around.

"Well, I found it curious that he refused to tell me what ye were discussing, especially if it was nothing more than going for a hike. But ye know Da. He's always so helpful, and though he didn't want to tell me what ye were up to, in the end I managed to convince him to tell me just a wee bit more."

Iain's temper flared, but he resisted the urge to pummel his brother. "I don't know what ye're implying, but ye've caused enough problems. And I'm not going to let ye ruin my time with Cat. Now if ye don't mind, take yer sorry arse back home and stay out of trouble. I'm tired of cleaning up yer messes."

Malcolm got to his feet and brushed past Iain, knocking into him with his shoulder. "This is far from over, Iain."

His brother left, slamming the door behind him. Iain could have strangled him, but didn't want to get into it with Cat there.

Cat. She must be mortified.

He shook his head, still annoyed. "I'm sorry ye had to see that. My brother forgets that his actions have an effect on the people around him—though I'm not sure he really cares either way."

"Trust me; I know what families can be like." She slipped her arms around his waist and looked up at him. "Don't let him get to you. We had a great day and got a lot done, yeah? We're one step closer, Iain."

"You're right." There was no point in letting his brother ruin things for him. Yet they might already be in a world of trouble. "Let me call my Da so I can set this aside. I need to know what he's already told my brother. Malcolm may be an arse and an idiot with most things, but he's also clever and I don't want him figuring out that we're looking for the Highlander's Hope."

She nodded. "Take your time. I'll get us a cup of tea to warm up."

He called his father's mobile phone but no one answered. He then tried his brother's home, but still couldn't get through to his father. He was likely down at the pub or taking a walk around the city and had forgotten his phone. He tried the cell again, and left a message. Hopefully his father would return his call before his brother got back to Edinburgh. He'd rather not have Malcolm around to eavesdrop again.

Not wanting Cat to fumble around the kitchen as she tried to find things, he headed over to give her a hand. "No luck getting a hold of him. I'll try him later."

She stood at the stove, throwing him a glance over her shoulder, her mahogany hair cascading down to a perfectly curved rear. "Still waiting for the kettle to boil."

He wrapped his arms around her waist, sidling up to her from behind and pulling her close. By the gods, he wanted her and was tempted to let her know just how much. Instead he kissed the slope of her neck and then, letting her go, leaned up against the kitchen table.

She turned and slipped into his arms, nestling between his legs, so it was all he could do to concentrate on what she was asking him. "Do you think your brother knows what we're up to?"

"At this very moment, I don't care." He wanted to kiss her, but she looked distracted. "Aye, love, I think there's a good chance he does know. My father wouldn't betray a confidence, but my brother's good at manipulating him and talking him around in circles. He could very well have told Malcolm without ever intending to. I'm sorry."

"He wouldn't do anything to jeopardize our search though, would he? If he mentions it…" Her brow creased with worry, making him want to curse his brother to the seven hells.

"I don't think he would, love, but… he's an arse." He let out a weary sigh, wondering how to contain the situation before it got out of control.

"Iain, if he tells anyone about this, we're screwed. News like this spreads like wildfire. Half the treasure hunters out there and every Scottish nationalist will come looking, and they're not going to care that this is your property, nor will they be nice about it."

"I'll talk to my father, and if it comes to it, I'll also speak to Malcolm. But I don't want ye worrying about this until we know it's a problem."

She turned away from him and took the kettle off the burner before pouring the steaming water into the pot with several teabags. "We won't be able to keep this a secret for long. And even if the necklace isn't anywhere near here, people are going to assume it is, or they'll assume we have it. We need to find it, Iain."

"Then that's what we'll do. We're on the right track, Cat. It's only a matter of time before we find the clue that'll lead us to the Hope." He twined his fingers with hers, needing to ease the tension between them.

As if finding a new determination and confidence, she pulled herself upright. "You're right. We're going to find it—I'll be damned if I'm going to let James or your brother mess this up."

Iain had to laugh. "I pity the man who stands in yer way, love."

She poked him playfully in the chest. "You think I'm kidding, but I'm not."

"Only a fool would stand between you and one of yer finds." He wrapped an arm around her waist and pulled her close, his self-control slipping when she was so feisty. "And I'm no fool."

When she looked up at him with a sultry smile, his heart tripped over itself with need. "No, you're not. It's one of the things I like about you."

"So ye *do* like me then? And here I thought ye just couldn't resist my good looks and charms."

"You're pushing it, MacCraigh." She laughed, slapping his chest.

He rubbed his chest, pretending. "That hurt, lass. Ye don't know yer own strength."

She quirked an eyebrow at him with a teasing smile that made his jeans feel two sizes too small. "You best behave yourself then."

"Aye? And if not?"

"You might just find out." She headed for the door, looking over her shoulder enticingly.

He had to laugh, hoping beyond hope that he could get himself into some mischief.

"Do ye have those letters? I've yet to have a look at them." Iain went over to where Cat had lain down in front of the fire to study, the journals and any other reference materials she could get her hands on sprawled around her. Duncan had managed to stake his claim, curled up next to her, and refused to move under any circumstance.

"Right here." She handed him a manila envelope and stuck her nose back in the journal she was reading.

Iain shifted some things over and then grabbed a seat on the floor next to her, putting a gentle foot on Duncan and sliding him over. That got him a doggie glare, which he proceeded to ignore. There was still a lot of ground to cover, between the journals, paintings and letters, but at least it was a doable task.

He pulled the letters out and quickly flipped through them while leaning back on the base of the sofa, his long legs stretched out in front him. "These are in Scots Gaelic." He looked at Cat in question.

"I forgot to mention it. I think it was to help them mask the clues further."

"And ye're able to read this?" He held up the letters.

"Can't you?" Her smug grin was laced with humor.

He leaned over and kissed her nose. "Aye, I can—though I don't exactly use it a lot. How did you manage to pick it up?"

"Scottish father, Irish mother. There was no escaping it, though I sort of know a mish-mash of the two Gaelic languages rather than anything proper. It's enough to get by, though it's another reason I want you to take a look."

"Brothers or sisters?" He really didn't know much about her. Didn't matter though. He liked what he did know.

"*Four* older brothers. Needless to say, dating was a nightmare."

"I can only imagine. Guess I better be on my best behavior. " Iain knew how protective he was of his sister, and doubted her brothers were any different.

She sat up and sidled next to him, tucking herself in at his side. "Read. We can be bad later."

"Bad? I thought I was supposed to be behaving myself?" He had to wonder why he thought her so prim and proper before. Little Miss Librarian. Maybe it was those cursed hairclips.

"Or... we could just get it out of the way."

His heart nearly stopped when she turned and straddled his lap, his hands automatically moving to her hips before he could give it a thought. "Cat, what are ye doing?"

Her lips curled into a lazy smile as she nuzzled him and nipped at his lips. "I like you, MacCraigh. A lot. And I don't say that often—nor do I normally let things get in the way of my studies and research." She nipped at him again. "I'm making an exception for you, Iain. Don't disappoint me."

His voice all but caught in his throat. "I'll try not to."

He ran his hands down her back as her mouth found his in a hungry kiss, their bodies pressed together, her hips shifting against his. Every nerve in his body awakened to her touch, the scent and taste of her filling his head so he was left dizzy with need. She nipped at his neck, adding yet another layer to the sensations he was feeling, his skin tingling so it was all he could do to keep from taking her then and there.

She yanked her sweater off and his heart nearly stopped. By the gods, she was beautiful. He cupped her face in his hands and kissed her as if she alone could sustain him, as if she was the air he breathed and the blood in his veins. Needing to feel her skin against his, he rid himself of his tee. He fisted her hair and gently pulled her head back so he could trail kisses down the slope of her neck.

"Please, don't stop on our account. I like to watch."

Iain shifted Cat off his lap and behind him in one quick move, turning to take in the threat, a rage consuming him. James—and his brother.

"What the hell, Malcolm? What is he doing here?" Why his brother was back, and with James no less, was beyond him. At least Cat had managed to get her sweater on.

"Found yer friend." It became clear Malcolm had been drinking. "We had a nice long talk and he's going to help me."

"Help ye with what?" Dread washed over Iain, as Cat grabbed his hand.

"With finding the Highlander's Hope, of course."

Chapter Eleven

"**Y**OU BASTARD." CAT lunged at James, but Iain grabbed her around the waist and held tight. Probably a good thing, since she was a heartbeat away from murder. She really thought she'd be successful in her search this time and would get the credit she deserved.

"Get him out of here, Malcolm. He isn't welcome here—and neither are you." Iain was bristling, and Cat was worried it'd soon come to fists. Even Duncan was on his feet, adding to the chaos with barks and growls.

"I have just as much right to be here as you do, Iain—and just as much right to the Highlander's Hope. I think ye forget that as long as Da's alive and doesn't mind having me around, it's my home too."

"A home ye'd be happy to gamble away. Ye even dragged our father into yer mess. Do ye want me to tell him how his investment's turned out? Do ye really think ye'll be welcome in his home when he finds out ye lied and manipulated him? Put our entire family in jeopardy just so ye could have a bit of fun? Get out. Now."

Iain moved towards the two men, clearly not in the mood to have his brother or James sticking around.

"This isn't over, Iain." Malcolm turned to go, but James lingered.

"I knew you were hiding something, Cat. Pity you didn't come to me first. I could have helped you—could have included you in the find."

Cat laughed in his face. "As if you'll find it without my help. Go home, James."

Iain and Duncan moved closer, and it was enough to get James moving. With the door locked behind their intruders, the gravity of what had just happened hit Cat like a fist to the gut.

She told herself it didn't matter. They would find the necklace first, and even if they didn't, it was just a necklace.

Yet it wasn't. It was the Highlander's Hope. The find of the century— *her* find.

Her eyes burned with threatening tears as she desperately tried to curse them away. She wouldn't let James get to her—except that he already had.

"I'm sorry, love." Iain pulled her into his arms and held her tight, kissing the top of her head. "I'll not let them back onto the estate, Cat. They won't get close enough to find it."

"What choice will you have?" She swiped at a tear that escaped, and steeled herself against any others, refusing to let them fall. "Malcolm knows we were at the loch and were asking about the Bleeding Heart. And there's no way to know if they're out in the hills wandering about. It's too large an estate to monitor."

"They still don't know enough to find it—and without the journals and the paintings, they won't stand a chance." He tilted her chin up so she'd have to look at him. "I'll have all the locks changed first thing tomorrow."

Now more than ever it felt like there was a clock ticking down to the end, and she wasn't going to make it. "We need to get back to the letters and journals."

She turned to go, but he gently grabbed her arm. "Leave it for the night, Cat. Clear yer head first, get a good night's rest, and then we'll start fresh in the morning."

She shook her head, looking over at all their research sprawled out across the library. "Iain, time's running out. We need to find it."

"Ye need a break, Cat. Ye're too worked up over this, and it won't do ye any good."

She shook her head no, her body still tense. "I'm too worked up to get any rest or to let it go. I can't."

"It's yer choice, but I don't like to see ye so upset."

Not wanting him to worry about her, she slipped her arms around his waist, and leaned her head on his still-bare chest, his skin hot against her cheek. Having him so close, she was more than a little tempted to vent her anger and frustration in a more productive way. Maybe pick up where they left off.

She kissed his chest and then the hollow of his neck, eliciting a moan of need from Iain, which happily resulted in some of her anger slipping free. Giving in to her emotions and desires, she bit his neck, while her hands moved to his hips, pulling him close.

"Cat... this isn't exactly what I had in mind for romancing ye."

"You were going to romance me? I like that." He was so sweet. And with a body like a Greek god. Handsome and smart too. It'd be a pity to let a jerk like James ruin her night—and she'd be damned if she was going to let him. All that anger? She could easily turn it to heat.

She kissed Iain. Hard. Taking all he had to offer, pulling away only long enough to comment between kisses. "Next time. We can do the romantic thing next time. Right now? I don't want to have to think."

"Aye, love. As ye wish." With his kisses deepening, he lifted her off her feet, her legs wrapping around his waist as he carried up the stairs and to his bedroom.

She slammed the door shut behind them and then pulled off her sweater, as he landed them on the bed. It had been far too long since she'd been with anyone, and after all that'd happened, she desperately needed Iain. Good thing he was more than willing.

He undid her bra with an experienced flick, his mouth closing around her nipple, her back arching in response as she held him to her. He made her forget her worries and anger, as if there was nothing else that mattered but the two of them.

His scent filled her head and stoked her passions, as she desperately slipped out of her jeans, and then helped free him of his remaining garments. Never had she wanted anyone more.

Her breath caught as he covered her in kisses, their bodies coming together so there was nothing but skin and flesh. Nothing but the beating of hearts and the joining of souls.

Cat woke up tangled in Iain's arms, with memories of their night together fresh on her mind. She didn't have a single regret.

Spinning around, she gave him a quick kiss as he stirred, his eyes refusing to open even as he kissed her back. "I'm going to make a pot of coffee, and then get back to the journals. Feel free to sleep in."

He gave her a grunt in response and then was asleep once more. Her lips slowly curled into a smile as she took him in—his dark curls and the start of a scruffy beard, muscular arms and long legs. She'd be happy to look at him all day—except she had the Highlander's Hope to find. Throwing on a pair of sweats and a tee, she headed downstairs, grabbed her jacket and let Duncan out.

The temperature had dipped, and a fierce wind was coming in from the ocean. She knew they weren't far from the water, though she'd yet to see it. Maybe Iain would take her—though not until it warmed up a bit. Now chilled to the bone, she called out to Duncan so they could head back in.

Probably chasing rabbits. She called out to him again, and then wandered in the direction he'd run off in. The last thing she needed or wanted was to lose Iain's dog. Continuing to call his name, she wandered further into the woods, trying not to get snagged on the branches and brush.

There was movement up ahead, and she started to call out, when she realized it wasn't Duncan. There were two men—and they didn't exactly look like hikers going for a stroll. She slowly let go of the branches she was holding aside, and started to back up when she came up short.

A blinding pain seared through her brain and everything went black as she hit the ground.

Cat fought back against the hands that held her as she came to, her head yet to clear, a scream trying to escape her lips.

"Cat, it's me. Iain. Open yer eyes, love." There was panic in his voice.

She fought her way through the fog, finally managing to focus on his worried face. He pulled her into his arms and held her close, before pulling away enough to look at her. "Ye've got a lump on yer head the size of an egg, and ye may have a concussion. Try yer best to hold onto me. I'm going to get ye out of here."

She nodded and held on as he lifted her into his arms and carried her out of the woods and back to his home. Everything was hazy as she tried to recall what happened. "Duncan… where is he?"

"He's right here, love. It was his barking that led me to ye." Once inside, he laid her down on the sofa in the sitting room and then took a seat next to her. "Who did this? Did ye see them?"

"I saw two men ahead of me, but there must have been a third person, since I got hit from behind." And that was some hit—her head was killing her.

"We need to get ye seen by a doctor. I'll also need to report this to the authorities. It was one thing when it was James snooping around, but I'm not going to tolerate ye being attacked." His brows were drawn together, his muscles taut.

She wished she could set his mind at ease, but the truth was they could very well be in serious danger now. "I know you'll have to report the attack, but I don't think they'll be able to do much about it, since I didn't see who actually attacked me. As for the bump on my head, I should be fine with a bit of ibuprofen and a bag of ice."

He shook his head while looking away, anger and frustration lining his face. "I think it's best if ye leave for a while—go back to Cambridge. It's no longer safe here, and ye're more important than finding the treasure."

"I am *not* leaving, Iain. You can call the cops here and get security put in, but I'm not going anywhere without the Hope." She sat up, her head instantly making her regret it as pain shot across her temples.

"Cat, they might not be so gentle next time, and I'll be damned if I'm going to let ye get hurt again." When he cupped her cheek, she leaned against his palm. With a sigh, he shook his head and pulled her into his arms, holding her tight. "Ye scared the hell out of me, love. First I couldn't find ye, and then when I did… ye were just lying there, lifeless."

"We'll be more careful, okay? But we can't let them find the Hope. They won't care what happens to it, and it's too historically important for it to end up pawned off." Cat knew it would get sold to the highest bidder, likely hidden away in some private collection, never to be seen again.

"Are ye sure I can't talk ye into going someplace safe?" She gave him a look that said he'd be waiting a long time to get her to agree to *that* plan. "Fine. Then we stay together at all times, and we take absolutely no risks. Agreed?"

"Agreed." Her eyes were locked on his, but his gaze was so intense, she thought it might consume her.

He kissed her slow and sweet, nearly distracting her from the throbbing in her head. When his kisses slowed, he stayed close, nuzzling her. "Cat…"

"What is it?" She pulled away to get a better look at him, worried by what she saw. Worse still was that she didn't understand what had him looking so unsure.

He looked like he was going to say something more, but smiled tentatively instead. "It's nothing. I'm just glad ye weren't more seriously hurt."

The sound of the front door opening had Iain off the couch and moving towards the hall, grabbing a candlestick along the way. A shriek tore through the air, and then the sound of voices.

When Iain returned, it was an older lady by his side, a guilty look on his face as he returned his makeshift weapon back to its place. "Cat, I'd like ye to meet Mrs. Gordon. Mrs. Gordon, this is Dr. Catriona Ross. She's looking into our clan history."

She'd seemed to recover from her scare quick enough. "Ah! So this is the lass the whole town's been talking of. It's a pleasure to meet ye, my dear."

Cat got to her feet to greet Mrs. Gordon, but was overcome with dizziness, slinking back to the sofa. "I'm sorry, I've had a bit of a migraine, and it's still bothering me."

Iain came to her side, looking concerned once more. "Ye need to rest."

"I'll go get her a cuppa. Some tea and a drop of whisky should do the trick." Without waiting for an answer, Mrs. Gordon turned and left the room, her movements efficient despite her sturdy frame.

If they had one ally in this fight, Cat hoped it was her. "You should go and help her. Not to mention it would be the perfect time to see what she knows about the area and lore."

He pursed his lips in annoyance. "Ye know, ye have a one track mind. Ne'er mind that ye nearly got yer head bashed in."

"And you worry too much. Go see what you can find out. Shoo!" She waved him away, but instead of going he gave her a quick kiss.

"I'll be back with yer tea and information."

She watched him go, thinking she could easily fall head over heels for him. It'd be easy to think of him as nothing but a pleasant distraction while looking for the jewels, but she'd grown more attached to him than that. He was charming and sweet, smart and caring. Yet, once they found the necklace, she would be back off to Cambridge. And realistically, she couldn't imagine Iain would be interested in anything serious—certainly not once they'd put some distance between them.

She knew Iain was one of the most eligible bachelors in Scotland, and a confirmed player, none of his relationships lasting more than a few weeks. Even though he said this felt different, she'd be a fool to think it would last once she was home. She could, however, make the most of their time together, and try not to give it much thought.

She was there to the find the jewels and that was exactly what she'd do.

Chapter Twelve

I AIN LISTENED TO Mrs. Gordon tell her stories as they waited for the kettle to boil and the tea to steep. He'd heard the stories before, but now he was listening to the details with renewed interest, asking questions and doing his best to remember it all so he could return to Cat with the information he'd gathered.

Despite not knowing Cat long, he already knew how her face would light up as he relayed the stories, knew how she'd vibrate with that contagious energy and enthusiasm. No, he may not know all the little details of her life, but what he did know was the heart of her.

Mrs. Gordon had stopped talking at some point and now stood there looking at him with an all too knowing look on her face that spelled nothing but trouble for him. "So, the rumors are true then. I would have sworn on my life that they weren't. After all, ye've ne'er been one to fall for a lass—at least not longer than a week or two."

"Mrs. Gordon, that's not true."

She made a face. "Don't lie to me, Iain. I've ye known ye since ye were in nappies, and ye've had no more love or interest in those other women past dipping yer wick."

Mortified, Iain knew his face must be scarlet. "So what are the rumors saying then? Surely nothing that's true. Ye know better than to pay them any heed."

"Aye, I'd normally agree with ye. But now that I've seen ye? I'd ne'er have believed it if not for my own two eyes. Ye're in love, Iain MacCraigh." She smiled at him. "I only wish yer Ma had gotten the chance to see it. She always hoped ye'd find some happiness, and will rest easier now, bless her soul."

"I wish it were the case, since it breaks my heart to disappoint you and my dead mother, but ye're mistaken. I think Cat's lovely, but I am telling ye now—I'm not in love."

"Och, aye. If ye say so."

The blank look on her face made Iain want to curse and had his back going up. "I barely know her."

"Do ye now?" Her raised eyebrows and questioning glare made him feel like he was seven again after being caught fibbing about stealing a cake before tea. "Ye can try lying to me and to yerself, but I don't need yer words to tell me the truth."

Desperately needing to change the subject, he pulled out his wallet and grabbed his assistant's business card. "Ye haven't been away in ages. I want ye to go pay yer sister a visit for a few weeks—on me. Call Grant. He'll set ye up with a flight and spending money."

She was already shaking her head no. "She's all the way in Spain. It's too expensive, Iain."

"It's not too expensive, considering all ye do for us. I insist." The last thing he needed was for her to get stuck in the cross-fire with all that was happening, and with strangers wandering about hitting people over the head, he couldn't take the risk. He grabbed the tray of tea and biscuits. "And I insist ye start yer holiday now."

After he finally managed to hush her protests and get her out the door, he headed to see Cat, even though his enthusiasm was now dampened, Mrs. Gordon's words still haunting him. It was nonsense to think he'd fallen in love with Cat.

He'd only known the girl a week or two, and for half that time they'd driven each other to drink. Certainly, he liked her—a lot—but he wasn't the sort to fall in love, even if he was enjoying himself. His life was too complicated and busy. He'd already put his work on hold to deal with his brother's mess and to help Cat, but before long, he'd need to get back. Business deals didn't close themselves, and he had a company to run.

"Here ye are. Tea with and a side of ibuprofen." He settled the tray on the side table and managed a smile, while attempting to push Mrs. Gordon's words from his mind.

Yet he was fooling no one.

"What's wrong?" She took his hand in his, her eyes searching his face.

"Just worried about ye. How's yer head?" He brushed a dark curl from her face, wanting to kiss her, but knowing he'd only second guess himself now.

"Iain... what's going on?"

He got up and paced, needing to burn off some energy and frustration. "It's nothing. I just want to find the necklace so this can all be over with and we can get back to our lives. I know ye're trying yer best to find it, but it's gotten dangerous. And I've got work I need to get back to."

"Well, I'm sorry that I'm keeping you from it. I hadn't realized." She looked at him, confused and a bit hurt, which only made him feel worse about how he was acting.

Though he certainly wasn't in love with her, it didn't mean he had to be an arse. He sat by her side with a weary sigh, still unsure of what exactly they were doing. "I'm the one who should be apologizing. I'm just not good with this sort of thing, and frankly, I don't want ye getting the wrong idea."

"And what idea would that be, Iain?" Gone was the worry, now replaced by annoyance, since it was clear what he'd been referring to. "I think you're reading too much into what happened last night. But if you can't handle it, then that's fine. I'm more than happy to keep our relationship purely professional."

"Ye think I can't handle it, aye? And what about you?" His temper was up, fueled by uncertainty and pride.

"What about me? I thought we could have a bit of fun. Isn't that what you're normally looking for with all those women you date? My career and studies are my first priority, Iain, so don't go thinking I need a ring and a wedding dress just 'cause we had a quick romp."

"I didn't think it that quick." His lips quirked in a smile, his anger with her and their situation put on hold in the face of her dismissing him.

"No. I'll give you that. You took your time and were not only thorough, but rather accomplished." She bit her lip, her eyes locked on his—and then as if a switch had flipped, she dismissed him once more with a shrug. "Pity you can't handle it without getting all worked up over what it does or doesn't mean. And here I was thinking it'd be fun to have another go."

"Ye think I can't handle it?" He pulled her close, nuzzling her and nipping at her lips, needing to prove her wrong.

She put a finger on his chest and pushed him away, a smug look on her face. "I believe that's exactly what I said. Admittedly, I find it a bit odd. If the tabloids are to be believed, you've never gotten even remotely attached to the women you've been with in the past. Or were you not interested because they *did* want more from you?"

"So now ye think ye know me?" He wanted to tell her she was wrong, and yet she wasn't far from the truth, even if she had the wrong end of the stick. "Well, ye don't. I won't deny they were looking for more from me, but if ye think those women were remotely interested in me beyond my power and wealth, then ye're mistaken. Think what ye will of me,

Cat, because it doesn't matter. I just want to find the jewels so we can each be on our merry way."

With a teasing smile she leaned forward and whispered in his ear. "Are you sure that's *all* you want?"

Her breath sent a shiver of need through him, erasing his mind of any coherent thought so his primal instinct was the only thing in control. He found himself kissing her before he could think, and it took all the strength he could muster to stop, even though he still held her close, his cheek pressed against hers. "By the gods, woman, ye'd drive a man to drink."

She'd yet to pull away, so when she laughed, it tickled his skin. "Would I, now?"

"Aye, ye would." He took a deep breath, hoping to clear his head of her scent, a mixture that reminded him of the tropics and lazy days on a hot beach—lime and coconut, salt and sun-kissed skin. "And have ye forgotten? Ye've got a head injury."

"I was hoping you'd distract me from it. Pity you're not interested."

He just shook his head and laughed at himself for thinking he had any control over the situation. Never before had he been such a fool. The woman left him dizzy, as if she'd blindfolded him, spun him around and then sent him off staggering as he desperately tried to remain upright.

Trying to regain some ground and get his bearings, he decided to change the subject to more neutral territory. "So are ye going to continue being a pain in my arse or do ye want to know what Mrs. Gordon had to say about the local lore?"

She gave him a quick peck on his cheek and then sat back. "Though I'm tempted to keep harassing you, I'm more interested in what you found out."

"Hmph. I thought ye might be." He picked up her legs and sat back on the sofa, letting them drape across his lap. "There are rumors of more tunnels. Better yet, they were supposedly used during Culloden, but were sealed off not long after. No one's really bothered to go looking for them, since there'd be no real reason to."

"But we know of a reason." Her eyes were alight, and her body thrummed with an excitement he wanted to make good use of. "I don't suppose she knew the location of the tunnels."

"Well, she'd heard stories about this home being used to hide and move weapons and men during the uprising or just after." He couldn't help but smile.

"You mean to tell me the tunnels could be hidden right underneath this home?" She leaned forward and grabbed his arm.

"Could be—or close enough near the house." He sighed, knowing what he had to say next would do absolutely nothing to deter her. "It might also be in a part of the home that's no longer safe."

The damned girl was all but vibrating in anticipation. "Did she have any other information? Though that's a damned good start."

"Cat, ye do realize ye've been accident-prone since ye got here. The last thing I need is for ye to be traipsing through a part of the home that's ready to collapse. With yer luck, it'd land right on that thick skull of yers."

"You know it'd likely bounce right off." She laughed but he didn't find it amusing. "Iain… you do realize you give off mixed signals."

"*I* give off mixed signals?" His temper sparked. "Just 'cause I don't want to fall in love with ye, doesn't mean I want to see ye get yer head bashed in—*again!*"

"So is that the problem, then? You don't want to fall in love with me?" Her mood had gone from lively to sober, all in the span of a heartbeat.

He dropped his head in his hands, frustrated and struggling to find the right words. "I barely know ye. The last thing I should be doing is falling in love with anyone. And that doesn't mean ye're not a lovely, intelligent, and utterly annoying woman. I'm just not looking for that sort of thing."

"And you think *I'm* looking for something serious? Just because I agreed to date you in earnest rather than pretend, doesn't mean I'm looking for a wedding ring." Her laugh made him want to silence her with a hard kiss. "Listen to me, Iain. I like you. And last night? I thoroughly enjoyed myself. But don't get yourself in a tizzy thinking I want anything more than a bit of fun. I've tried doing the whole serious relationship thing, and it's not something I'm interested in—at least not when I have so much else going on in my life."

He shook his head as the pieces fell into place and he started to make sense of it all. "Cat… I'm nothing like James."

She let out a weary sigh. "No. You're not. But it doesn't matter, Iain. You've made it clear you're not interested, and neither am I. So what exactly are we arguing about?"

"I wish I knew, love."

⊠ ⊠ ⊠

Iain called his assistant and had Grant find a security company that could handle putting in a system for a place as big and difficult to secure as his family home. Luckily, he was also able to get in touch with his father, and though his father was fine, his brother had yet to make it back to Edinburgh—which only made him worry further.

That was his next call, though it went straight to Malcolm's voice-mail. Iain cursed, unsure about what to do. If James and Malcolm were now working together—and knew about the Hope—then things were even more dire. And who were the men that had attacked Cat? Had James and Malcolm opened their mouths while at the pub and been overheard?

How the bloody hell had they even figured out that he and Cat were looking for the Hope? He supposed it made sense if familiar enough with the local history, and it's not like he himself had a hard time figuring it out.

Iain debated calling the police to tell them about the attack, but knew there was little to go on, and didn't want to draw even more attention to what they were doing. If the tabloids started sniffing around, there'd be no chance of keeping it a secret—and tabloids always kept track of police reports. They would just have to be more careful.

He found Cat sitting cross-legged in front of the paintings. And finally—no cursed hair clips. Her long dark hair had been twisted and braided loosely, before cascading down her back in a spill of curls, the mahogany color picking up glints of red in the light. It was as if she'd wandered out of a fairytale, despite wearing a long, oversized sweater that hung off one shoulder to expose a tank below, knit leggings and shearling boots.

It suited her—far more than the buttoned-up look she'd first worn. He had to laugh. Maybe it had been a ploy to throw him off guard. To make him think she was prim and proper rather than the smart and feisty vixen she really was. His lips pursed at the thought, and he knew it was partly because she had no interest in pursuing something more permanent with him—even though he kept telling himself he wasn't interested in anything of the sort either. He felt like a child, interested in a toy only after being told he couldn't have it.

Worried she'd see his thoughts and emotions written all over his face, he went to the fireplace and started to layer the wood and kindling. He liked the routine of building a fire, and the smell of it always pulled at something ancient within him, as if his soul was tied to this land and place, to the ways of old. He'd tried to live elsewhere, given that the Scottish highlands weren't exactly a business Mecca, and ended up miserable.

Feeling more calm and in control now that he had a roaring fire warding off the October chill, he sat down on the floor next to Cat. "How's yer head?"

"It's still sore if I touch it, but the ibuprofen's kicked in so my headache's gone."

"I spoke with my father. He promised he spoke not a word about the necklace to anyone." At least his father was safe. Iain had been worried when he couldn't get in touch with him.

She tilted her head towards him, her brows drawn in question. "Then how did Malcolm and James know about it?"

"That's exactly what I want to know. It could be that Malcolm figured it out, if James told him you were here to research a find. Not that it really matters now that they know." There was something nagging at the corners of his brain, but he couldn't quite figure it out.

She turned towards him, her legs still curled under her. "Again, it just means we need to find it first. I know your brother has just as much right to it as you do, but if he's teamed up with James, there's no way I'm stepping aside."

Anger bubbled within him, his brother's mess too big to easily ignore. Everything was on the line. "Trust me when I tell ye, my brother has no claim, and if there's anyone ye should be worrying about getting the jewels, it's him. He'd sell his first-born for a few quid and not give it a second thought."

"Come on then." She stood up, took his hands, and hauled him to his feet. "Let's go find us some tunnels."

Her smile pushed away at the dark cloud that was consuming him. "I'm only going to take ye if ye promise me ye'll be careful, *and* ye'll do as I say. If I tell ye it's too dangerous and we need to turn back, ye'll not argue with me, aye?"

The glint in her eye told him he was in trouble. "Och, aye. I promise to do just as ye say and obey yer every word, m' laird."

He was surprised to find her mock Scots could pass for the real thing, when he remembered that her father was Scottish. He bit back his laugh and furrowed his brow, trying his best to be stern with her. "I'm going to hold ye to it, Cat."

A single brow perked up, mischief alight in those green eyes of hers, while she ran her hands up his chest and around his neck to whisper in his ear. "My dear, you make a girl want to misbehave."

His breath caught at the thought, his heart pounding. "Bloody hell."

CHAPTER

Thirteen

C AT FOLLOWED IAIN through the ruined part of the home, the stone walls climbing up to an open sky, the roof long gone. Moss and vines clung to the surface, the earth's attempts to reclaim its own, while still-standing arches and window openings harkened to what once had been.

Though it didn't come close to rivaling the famous castles and manor homes in size, there was something about the place. The details and beauty of line and form spoke of an elegance still not lost, despite the crumbling and decaying effects of time and the harsh Scottish elements.

Cat thought she could spend an eternity exploring the manor and its grounds, and never find all the secrets that lay hidden away, waiting to be discovered. It was with a pang that she thought of her time here soon coming to an end, but she quickly pushed those thoughts away, knowing it did no good to dwell on the inevitable.

"Did Mrs. Gordon give any indication as to where the tunnels might be?"

"Just beyond these open ruins is a part of the home that's in better shape, though it's cut off from the rest of the home because of the roof collapse here. It's still not in great condition though, and because it still has its roof, it's even more dangerous than this section here. We'd discussed tearing it down, or building some parts of it back up, though we never came to any final decisions."

Cat's foot slipped on the algae-covered stones, but she managed to regain her balance before twisting an ankle or falling on her rear. Iain gave her a quick glance followed by an eye roll, since he clearly thought her accident prone. Where he'd get such an idea, she hadn't a clue.

Iain grabbed her hand and held on, supporting her when she needed it. "Once we're done here, I'd like to go back to the tunnels by the Bleeding Heart. If not today, then tomorrow. I don't feel like we explored it thoroughly."

"Isn't there something we can use to find the caves? Would it be sonar?" She didn't know much about these things.

"My assistant is looking into what options would be best, and will have them shipped here in the next few days." He squeezed through an opening in a wall, and then gave her a hand climbing through.

"You didn't tell him what you needed the stuff for, did you?" That was the last thing they needed. One more person looking for the Hope.

"He's my assistant, Cat, not my BFF. I don't have to explain myself to him."

"He's not going to find it odd that you're looking for cave detection equipment?"

"And a metal detector."

She sighed. "Great."

His lips quirked into an amused smile. "Cat, it doesn't matter if he thinks it odd. He's my assistant. It's his job to do as I ask without giving it a second thought, and he's loyal. He'd not be my assistant otherwise."

"Does everyone always do as you say without questioning you?" She was sure that was the case when it came to his business at any rate.

"Obviously not, love. Ye've yet to listen to a single word I've said, and my brother's ne'er paid me any heed." He shook his head and ran a rough hand down his face. "Ye may think me arrogant, but he wouldn't be in any of the trouble he's in if he'd have just listened."

Cat had to wonder what sort of mess Malcolm had got himself into. It was clear, based on Iain's reaction, that it was serious. "I know I've offered before, but… if you want to talk, I'm here, Iain."

"I'm afraid it'd only remind me of the mess he's in and annoy me further." He brushed a stray curl from her eyes, and then cupped the back of her neck and pulled her in close for a quick kiss. "I do appreciate yer offer, but dinnae fash yerself, love. I'll manage just fine."

"I hope you're right." With a sigh, she slipped her arms around his waist, resting her head on his chest as he held her close. "I know I have no right, and you can manage just fine, but you have me worried."

"Och, love, that's the last thing I want." He kissed the top of her head and then took her hand. "Shall we continue? I believe this is the room Mrs. Wallace mentioned."

Cat looked around, happy to leave her worries behind, if for just a bit. Most of the walls were still intact, despite parts of the roof missing. From what was left of the room, it appeared to be more utilitarian—a kitchen perhaps? She started to wander away from Iain's side. "There could be an entrance hidden in the floor or the walls."

"Just be careful. There's rubble everywhere, and if there's a tunnel below, I don't want ye falling through."

Unable to resist flirting with him, she threw him a teasing smile over her shoulder. "What are the chances of that happening?"

She barely had the words out when a wooden plank gave way, gouging her leg from calf to knee. Iain was at her side in a heartbeat, muttering curses under his breath as he helped her extract herself, leaving her boot behind in the hole. He carried her over to a large stone and sat her down.

"Let me see." Carefully, he pulled her pant leg up and out of the way, and let out a huge sigh of relief. "We'll need to disinfect it when we get back, but it's mainly just a bit of scraped skin and a few splinters. Yer boot saved ye from the worst of it. I swear, Cat. Ye're going to be the death of me. Are ye always this bad or is it just around me?"

"I think you've somehow managed to amplify how accident-prone I am." Pulling down her pant leg, she gave him a reassuring smile, hoping it'd work. "Don't look so upset. It's just a scrape. I'm fine."

"You're fine *this time*." His curses switched to Gaelic—never a good sign, as far as Cat was concerned, having been on the receiving end of it more than once when she'd exasperated her father.

"I promise to be more careful, but right now, I want my boot back and I want to know what sort of hole my foot fell into."

He shook his head, his entire body tense. "Ye have a one-track mind, woman. Does it not matter that ye're constantly getting hurt?"

"Iain... what do you want me to do? I'm here to find the necklace, and will do whatever it takes. I'm not going to let those jerks scare or bully me out of finding it, and I'm certainly not going to let bumps and bruises slow me down." She grabbed his shirt, resisting the urge to shake him as her emotions rose to the surface, refusing to be beaten back.

Suddenly, everything felt as if it was slipping out of control. First James and Malcolm, and now total strangers, all trying to get to the Hope. The last thing she could afford to do was slow down and take things easy.

Her eyes burned with threatening tears, but she refused to let her emotions get in her way. "You're not going to stop me, Iain, and I'm not leaving until I find the Hope. Do you hear me?"

"Aye, love. Hush." He pulled her into his arms, and held her tight, murmuring to her in Gaelic until she'd calmed down. "I'm not trying to stop ye, Cat. But each time ye get hurt and brush it off like it's of no consequence, it worries me that ye're not being careful enough, and ye're taking too many risks. We'll find the necklace. But I don't want it to be with our dying breath."

With a large exhale, she rid herself of the tension eating away at her, knowing he was right. It just meant he cared—and that was nice. She went up on her toes and gave him a kiss on the cheek. "You're a sweet man, Iain MacCraigh. It's a good thing I have you around to keep me safe."

"A sweet man, aye? Just don't let that get around. I have a reputation to uphold. You know… playboy, ruthless businessman, and what was it ye called me on the day we first met? Ah yes, arrogant jerk."

She had to laugh. The two of them certainly had come a long way since he'd nearly run her over. "Who knew you'd be such a contradiction. I'll admit, I'm glad I've been given the opportunity to find that out."

"Are ye really?" He twined his fingers with hers and brought them to his lips, a sparkle in his eyes. "Then let's hope ye manage to live long enough to make the most of it."

The way he looked at her would have any woman swooning into his arms. Pity it would eventually have to come to an end. She supposed she could make the most of their time together—or concentrate on work instead. "Are you ready to check out that hole then?"

"Aye, love. But first things first." He got to his feet, went over to where her foot had gone through the board, and pulled away at some of the rotten wood so he could reach in and grab her boot. He held it up victoriously before sliding it onto her foot. "Not exactly a glass slipper, is it?"

"Well, last I checked, I wasn't exactly Cinderella."

He laughed. "Ye know ye want to say it—and I'm not exactly Prince Charming."

Her lips tugged into a smile. "Truth is, you're pretty damn close. Not something I ever anticipated."

"That's because, like so many others, ye underestimated me, Cat." He stood up and, taking both her hands in his, pulled her to her feet. "But I don't mind, love. It's how I'll win."

Somehow she'd managed to awaken his competitive side, and it now felt like he was getting ready to eat her alive. She perked an eyebrow at the thought, her lips curling into a seductive smile. Could be far too entertaining—and she was always up for a challenge.

"Ready to go exploring, then?" She looked up into those piercing blue eyes and thought him a worthy opponent.

"Aye, love. Just watch yer step this time. Wouldn't want ye to do yerself an injury when the fun's just starting."

They squatted in front of the hole and removed the debris that had fallen onto the floor from the ceiling above. After a good ten minutes, they managed to expose what seemed to be a door in the floor. The hinges were rusted through, though they remained intact when Iain pulled it open. He grabbed the flashlight and shone it down the stone steps that led into the darkness. Cat's heart thundered at the possibilities. The jewels had to be close by. It might be wishful thinking, but she had to stay positive. Research would never get done with a pessimistic attitude.

Iain handed her a flashlight, and slowly went down the steep staircase before turning around and giving her a hand. The passageway was narrow, dark and damp, and Cat had to suppress a shiver as Iain swiped at the cobwebs.

He stopped short. "It's not a tunnel, Cat. It ends right here."

She tried her best to not let it get her down, and yet a weary sigh escaped. "It was likely used as a hiding hole during the uprising and in the years after. Just means there's a good chance there are other tunnels around."

Iain held the flashlight up and started to take a closer look at the walls. "I keep thinking there's more to these tunnels and rooms than we can actually see. Not that I expect us to press a button and have a wall swing open to reveal a hidden chamber, but... something."

She had to laugh. "I know, right? And trust me, I've been on enough of these searches to know better, yet I still feel around for cracks in walls and pull down on wall sconces. I guess I've watched far too many movies."

"You and me both." He pressed on the wall, shifting his hand around as he applied pressure and ran his fingers down the seams, before turning back to her with a playful grin. "It was worth a shot."

"We can keep looking. There might be another tunnel somewhere else in the ruins, or more clues in the paintings." She couldn't give in to her doubts, nor could she let James find the necklace. They just had to be persistent.

"Aye, love. Let's finish looking around here so we can check it off the list."

Cat started to head back when she startled to a stop, Iain coming short behind her. Voices could be heard in the ruins above them. With a tilt of her head towards the stairs, she motioned to Iain.

He quietly pushed past her while turning off the flashlight, his voice barely a whisper. "Get to the back of the room. Now. And no matter what happens, stay put."

CHAPTER Fourteen

IAIN'S MIND RACED. He had no weapon on him, and couldn't risk Cat getting hurt. He snuck towards the opening to get a better idea of what he was dealing with—and if it turned out to be Malcolm and James, he'd murder them both.

He could hear them. There were at least two men, maybe three. Scottish. And unless his brother was keeping quiet, he wasn't there. If they were the ones who attacked Cat, then the situation could be dangerous. Could he make his presence known and lead them away so Cat could escape, or would he just draw attention to her? Would it be better to just stay quiet and hope they didn't notice the steps?

Except for the fact that he was furious that they'd hurt Cat. They were on his land, in his home, and he'd be damned if he wasn't going to protect what was his.

Making use of his anger, Iain stalked up the stairs and pushed away any thoughts that he was doing the wrong thing. At the very least, he'd lead them away from Cat. He cleared the last step while quickly taking in the scene. Two men, about twenty feet away, one in his thirties, and another in his fifties.

"Ye better have a damned good explanation as to why ye're on my property and snooping around my home. And if I find out ye're the ones who attacked my guest, there'll be hell to pay." He tapped the long metal flashlight against his palm and moved towards them to draw their attention away from the room Cat was hiding in.

It was the older man who answered him. "The name's MacTavish, and this here's Campbell. Ye must be Callum's lad then. My apologies about the girl—that wasn't meant to happen, and the man responsible has been disciplined. She startled him, and he reacted on instincts that weren't very good."

"She could have been killed. And ye've yet to tell me what ye're doing here on my property." Iain took them in, wondering about his chances in a fight. If they remained unarmed, he thought he stood a fair chance, though the younger man was built like an ox.

"We're here because yer brother thinks the Highlander's Hope is on yer land, and ye know the legends, the symbolism—that Scotland will gain its independence when the Hope is found." He shrugged, even if his eyes sparkled. "And aye, they're just tales of old, but given the importance of the necklace, we can't have it falling into the wrong hands."

"Nationalists? Well, I fully support Scotland's independence, but I doubt any official group has condoned yer actions or the violence used, which leads me to believe ye're working on yer own. So don't go hiding against the Nationalist movement, when ye're no more than bullies." Iain scoffed, trying not to give anything away. His nerves were on edge—the men had closed the distance between them, splitting up, so he'd have a harder time keeping an eye on both of them.

"Those are some harsh words, lad." MacTavish looked annoyed, despite his lips curling into a smile.

"Well here are some more. If ye're hoping to find anything of value in what my brother's had to say, then ye don't bloody well know him. He's always been one to talk, and there's yet to be any truth to anything coming out of his gob. So the two of ye can piss off and if I see ye on my land again, ye'll be dealing with the police."

Campbell was big but he was slow, so when he charged forward, Iain sidestepped him and lunged at MacTavish, catching him at waist-height and knocking him off his feet before he had a chance to react. MacTavish hit the ground hard, but Campbell hadn't missed a beat. Pain erupted across Iain's back and knocked him to his knees when Campbell hit him with a wood plank. Another blow had Iain's vision erupting in a spray of light and darkness as he was knocked forward, his head swimming.

Iain managed to roll onto his back, hoping to catch the next blow, when Campbell's eyes rolled into the back of his head and he fell to the ground.

Cat stood there holding a rock in her hands, shaking. "He could have killed you. I had to. The cops... I called on my cell. They're on their way."

She dropped the rock and went to Iain's side, helping to steady him and get him on his feet. Iain turned to MacTavish, his head still swimming. "I suggest ye take yer friend and get the hell out of here. Next time I see any of ye on my land, I'll be armed and ye won't get a warning."

He could try and hold them for the cops, but truth was, he feared the attack would escalate, and he wouldn't be able to protect Cat. Better to let them go and let the authorities deal with them later.

MacTavish hauled Campbell to his feet as the man started to come to, blood pouring from a gash on his head. "If ye think this is over, ye're gravely mistaken."

Iain watched them go until he was sure they wouldn't be returning. Worried about Cat, he held her close. Adrenaline coursed through his body and left him overwhelmed and on edge, even if it wasn't enough to erase the pain. It could have easily been far worse though, and for that he was grateful.

"Thank ye, love." The poor girl was shaking like they'd fished her out of the loch in the middle of winter. Putting his arms around her, he held her tight, wishing she didn't have to go through any of this.

"He was going to kill you, Iain—and I nearly killed him."

"Hush, love. Don't go worrying yerself. I'll heal before long, and that bastard got no more than he deserved." Iain kept scanning the area, half expecting more men to come traipsing through the ruined walls. If they did, there'd be little he could do to fend them off. He felt like he'd been hit by a train, his back and shoulders battered and bruised. "Did ye really call the police?"

"No. I couldn't get any reception down in the hole, but thought it'd keep them from hanging around. But we should call the cops, Iain. This is totally getting out of control. I can't bear to think of what might have happened." She could barely hold his gaze for more than a second, and it made his heart ache.

He brushed her cheek and tried to get her to look at him. "Cat, we'll manage. And I don't want ye worrying about something that didn't happen. Let's just get back to the house for now. We'll sort it out."

"No, we won't. They could have killed you, damn it. And you know what? No necklace is worth that."

"Ye can't give up, Cat. Not when ye're so close. It's too important to ye." And that was the truth, even if he also had so much riding on the necklace. "We just need to be more careful. We'll take more precautions from now on, and I swear, I'll do all I can to protect ye."

She nodded, but didn't look at him as she started to head back. Her body was taut with coiled tension, and by the time they were back in the library, she'd barely given him a second glance.

When she did finally look at him, it was clear she was still struggling with what had happened. "I want you to see a doctor."

"I'll be fine, love. Don't worry." He took her hand in his, but she yanked it away.

"It will *not* be fine, Iain. How can you even say that after what just happened?" She shook her head, cursing under her breath as she started to pace the room. "You've been on my case about not being careful enough, but what about you, huh? You think it's perfectly fine to nearly get beaten to death, and then not even bother to have your injuries looked at."

The last thing he wanted to do was drag a doctor into this, but he found that, oddly enough, he actually cared about whether or not she was angry with him. "I'll have Angus take a look. There's no one else around, anyway, and while he's here, he can also take a look at yer head."

"Let me see." She motioned for him to take off his shirt. "I want to see how badly you've been injured, especially if you're thinking of only having a *vet* look at you."

He didn't protest too much, since she cared enough to be upset that he'd gotten hurt. His muscles screamed in protest as he tried to pull his tee over his head, grateful when she came to his aid. Taking care, she gingerly removed his shirt, and then stepped around him to look at the damage. When she sucked in her breath and said not a single word, he knew his back must already be bruised.

Turning to face her, he saw that her tears had spilled over, though there was more there—she was furious, and with an intensity that made him think that, for Campbell's sake, it was a good thing he was long gone.

"Hush, love. Dinnae fash yerself. I'm fine. It's just a few bruises." And maybe a cracked rib or two, though he thought it best to leave that part out. He pulled her into his arms and brushed her cheeks dry. "Angus will send me to a physician if he thinks I need to go."

She stepped out of his embrace and turned away, holding her arms across her chest as if to ward off a chill. "I think it'd probably be best if I got going."

It felt like the air had gotten knocked out of him. "Go where, Cat?"

"Cambridge. I need to get a new tire and then I'll be on my way." She wouldn't even look at him.

"Just like that?" He scoffed, his temper getting the better of him in the face of her leaving. "And here I thought ye were better than that. Go on then. Let MacTavish find it—or even better, James and my brother."

Iain expected her to turn around, ready for a fight. Or to turn around with a smug smile to say she knew he was baiting her but she'd prove him wrong and they'd find the jewels. And he hoped she would look at him with that fire in her eyes that erased all thoughts but her from his mind.

Yet she did none of those things.

"I should go check my email and let my assistant know I'm ok, and will be back in Cambridge in a few days' time." She headed for the door, but he'd be damned if she was going anywhere.

"Cat... ye can't go." He grabbed her arm and pulled her around. "We're too far into it to give up now."

Her face was flushed, and the fire in her eyes had returned, even if it was tainted with pain. "It's just a necklace, Iain. You get that, right? And though you may be willing to get your head bashed in over it, I'm not going to help you do it. Those men aren't like James and Malcolm—they're dangerous. And you bloody well know they're not going to stop until they get what they want."

"And ye think they'll leave just 'cause we've given up looking for it? Well, that's where ye're wrong, Cat. The only hope we have of keeping safe is to find the necklace before anyone else does. Once it's safely locked away and the find is made public, then there won't be any point to them threatening us." He didn't want to have to say it, but knew it might be the one thing to make her stay. "Ye're the one who brought this to my doorstep. My family and I are now under threat because of it, and I'll be damned if ye think ye can just leave without first putting things right. None of us are safe until it's found. Not me and my father, nor you, even if ye flee to Cambridge."

At his accusation that she'd put them in harm's way, the blood drained from her face, leaving her freckles to stand out against now too-pale skin. He wanted to comfort her and tell her it wasn't her fault, but knew they'd both be better served if her hurt was turned to anger.

"Ye're staying put, Cat. Ye hear me? Once ye find the necklace, ye can take yerself off to wherever ye bloody want to go—but not before that."

Anger sparked in her eyes, but there was also a keen intelligence there, and he knew, despite her anger, she was not fooled. "I'm sorry that I dragged you into this, Iain, but short of tying me up, I'm going."

Her words had his control slipping as he pulled her to him and nuzzled her, his arm wrapped around her waist to keep her from escaping. "Don't tempt me, love. It'd be a lovely sight to see ye trussed and squirming."

"This isn't funny, Iain." She pried herself from his embrace, and with a shake of her head, turned to go.

Well, he'd be damned if he was going to let her walk out on him without giving it a second thought. He pulled her around, ignoring the tears that welled up in her eyes. "You're not leaving, Cat. Not until this is over."

"I'm sorry. It was a mistake to involve you. You see that, right? I can't bear to have you get hurt again." She struggled to get free, but he held on tight, as the tears finally spilled over and rolled down her cheeks. "Let go of me, Iain. I can't do this."

"Ye can and ye will. We'll find the Hope, aye? Cause they're not going to go away, love. We've no other choice." He kissed her tears away until she stopped struggling and let out a weary shudder. He hated to see her so upset, but hoped he could turn her mood around. "So… are ye going to stay or do I need to get the rope?"

She let out a laugh, which helped to ease his worries. "I think we might both like that far too much—and you're still injured."

Relief washed over him. He brushed a curl from her face, his touch lingering against the warmth of her skin. "Does that mean ye're staying?"

She wrapped her arms around his waist and leaned her head against his bare chest, sending his heart racing. "I guess I'll have to for now. Someone's got to have your back."

"Well, I'm glad it's you, love."

The police had come and gone, taking their report and promising to look into the matter. In the meantime, they had new company and problems to contend with.

A sharp pain set Iain's nerves on fire as Angus poked and prodded. "Bloody hell. Could ye be a bit more gentle?"

Angus finished his examination and tossed Iain his shirt, his mood serious. "Ye've got severe bruising and may also have a cracked rib, though that should heal on its own. What the hell happened to the two of ye? Her head, yer back. This was no accident, Iain, and I'd appreciate some honesty."

Iain glanced at Cat in question, knowing the decision was hers to make. She nodded. "Might as well—enough people already know, and for once, I'd rather have it be someone who's on our side."

Iain let out a sigh of relief, happy to no longer have to keep things from Angus. "We've been looking for the Highlander's Hope. Cat thinks it was last in the hands of one of my ancestors who hid it somewhere on our estate."

Angus let out a low whistle of surprise. "I can't believe it. The Highlander's Hope, aye? I thought that was nothing more than legend."

Cat shook her head no, her eyes alight, clearly in her element. It made Iain smile to see her like that, happy that the day's uncertainty was behind them. "My research shows that it did indeed exist, but got lost or hidden along the way."

Angus grabbed a seat next to Iain and across from Cat. "That still doesn't explain what happened to the two of ye."

"Unfortunately, her ex and my eejit brother figured out what we've been up to, without taking into consideration that they could easily be overheard. Somehow, a bunch of thugs caught wind of what they were discussing, and decided to come looking for it." Iain slowly worked his way into his shirt, trying his best to ignore the pain.

"And that means it's gotten dangerous." Angus sat forward and propped his elbows on his knees. "What are ye going do? They'll likely not stop until they get what they want."

That was exactly what Iain was worried about. "It's why we need to find it—and soon."

"Don't know if I can be of any help, but I'm here should ye need me for anything." Angus sat back, his gaze shifting between the two of them. "So the two of ye?"

Iain knew what Angus was asking. "We thought it'd be best if people didn't know the real reason why Cat was here, and thought it'd be easy enough to hide behind a romantic involvement."

"Ye had me fooled, I'll tell ye." Angus looked at the two of them again with a tilt of his head, scrutinizing them, before giving her a smile. "Does that mean ye're single, then?"

Though Cat laughed and smiled at Angus, she threw Iain a furtive glance, as he attempted to squash the unexpected jealousy that sparked within him. "I can't imagine you're still single, Angus. Surely you already have someone who's head over heels crazy about you."

Angus turned to Iain, with his head cocked and a solicitous smile. "And here I thought we were being honest with each other. That's fine though. If ye don't want to tell me what's really going on between ye, I understand."

Iain groaned. It wasn't like he even knew what the hell they were doing. They'd spent last night together, and shared more than a few... moments, but he hadn't a clue what to call it. The honest truth was that he'd never had any reason or desire to call it anything at all with the other women he'd been with. But with Cat? He found he actually wanted to define what they had.

"All I can tell ye is that Cat is unlike any other woman I've met, and I'd consider myself damned lucky if she were to even give me a second glance." Iain found himself looking in her direction as he spoke the words.

When she looked away, his heart sank, leaving him to curse himself for being fool enough to care about her. How ironic that she was acting the way he normally did with the women he dated.

But then she surprised him.

"Don't listen to him, Angus. He knows damn well that I've been far from immune to his charms." She flashed her green eyes at him, and got to her feet. "I'm starving. Do you two want something to eat? I'm cooking."

Iain cocked his head, unable to refrain from teasing her. "That depends—can you manage it without cutting off a few fingers?"

She patted his cheek, a sly smile upon her lips. "See, Angus? Such charm. I don't know how anyone could resist."

CHAPTER Fifteen

AFTER THEIR MEAL, they retired to the library with a drink in hand. Cat showed Angus the paintings and the clues hidden in the brushstrokes, while Duncan sprawled at his feet hoping for a scratch. "Iain was the one who figured out that there were parts of the landscape that didn't belong. We checked it out, and there are tunnels leading from the loch to the Bleeding Heart, though we didn't find any flashing neon lights pointing to the necklace."

"We'll go back and take a more thorough look tomorrow. According to my Da, there are supposedly more tunnels near the ones we already explored. And then we still have to finish going through the ruins at the other end of the house." Iain turned to Angus. "Ye're welcome to join us. Ye can stay in one of the guest rooms if ye'd like."

"I'll come back mid-morning, if that suits ye. I've got a herd of sheep to vaccinate, and need to check in on a colicky horse." He checked his watch and got up with a stretch, when his eyes fell on one of the paintings. "What about this one here? Did ye notice, Iain? That tree is on the other side of the clearing, not near the rock face."

Cat and Iain both took a closer look, though Cat had no way of telling if what Angus was saying was true. Iain, however, started to nod. "Aye. I didn't notice at first, thinking it just another tree, but ye're right—that's the big oak with the splayed branches and carvings. And though there may have been a tree there at one point, there is currently no tree in front of those rocks."

"It could be another cave, if we're lucky." Cat tried to remain optimistic, and with this new information, it was easy to do.

Iain pulled her to him with a smile. "We've got to be close, love. It's only a matter of time."

"I hope so."

The day's attacks were still worrying her. Seeing Iain injured made it clear that Cat's feelings for him had gotten away from her, and things were now more serious than she'd wanted or anticipated. It'd be easy enough to tell herself that it was nothing more than a bit of fun when her life was too busy for anything serious, but she now suspected it'd be nothing more than a lie.

Ignoring her feelings for him might work. If there was one thing she was good at, it was burying herself in work so she wouldn't have to face her emotions—James had certainly given her enough practice doing just that.

But Iain was not James, and she wasn't sure she wanted to ignore the way he made her feel. Whether the feeling was entirely mutual, she didn't know. There was a definite attraction, yet he might not feel any different about her than he'd felt about the dozens of other women he'd dated. She'd like to think so, but she was also pretty realistic about who he was and the life he led, and knew better than to trust the words men spoke in the heat of the moment.

Angus said his goodbyes with a promise he'd be back late in the morning. While Iain saw him to the door, Cat curled up on the sofa with the love letters, desperately needing to distract herself from her own love life. She was curious to see if there were more clues or references that might stand out now that she had more pieces to the puzzle. With the letters set in chronological order, she noted that the letters between Nessa and Robert hadn't started out as love letters but rather a genuine friendship and deep affection after the death of Nessa's husband.

Cat set those early letters aside, knowing they predated the existence of the jewels. She'd go through them again, but only after she'd gone through the more pertinent correspondence.

"Any luck?" Iain sat down next to her, and pulled her legs into his lap.

"Nothing yet." She continued to scan the letters, quickly translating things in her mind, when she realized Iain had said something. "I'm sorry. What did you say?"

"I'm glad ye're staying."

"I am too, though…" She let out a sigh, cursing herself for going down this road. Why on earth she felt the urge to discuss her feelings for him was beyond her. "I've got to warn you, Iain. I don't know if I can keep up this thing we're doing without starting to fall for you."

"Ye're only *starting*? Bloody hell, woman, what's a guy gotta do?" His smile helped erase her worries, despite his mood becoming more serious. "Cat, if ye think I'm normally like this with other women, then ye're mistaken."

He shook his head with a sigh, not looking at her as he continued. "The thought of ye leaving – or worse, the thought of ye coming to harm—has my stomach in knots. Ye may only be starting to fall for me, love, but I'm already a goner."

Setting aside the letters, she turned back to him, her eyes locked on his, as she slipped her arms around his waist and he held her close. She kissed him with just a brush of her lips, while her head swam with uncertainty.

She took a good look at him. Bloody hell, he was handsome. She loved how his blue eyes stood out in contrast to his dark unruly hair, and that he'd let the stubble come in over his strong jaw.

With a deep breath, she steeled herself to be honest not only with him, but with herself. "The truth is, you scare me." The shock and concern in his eyes had her quickly trying to explain. "Not like that—not ever like that. But I'm not naïve, Iain. You don't get to be Scotland's most eligible bachelor by being in a committed long-term relationship, and I like you too much for this to be casual."

"Aye, I deserve that. But I swear things are different with ye, Cat." He brushed the back of his hand down her cheek and kissed her sweetly, a whisper of lips meeting in a promise of love and desire. "I don't want this to be casual, love. Ye mean too much. And I know it seems crazy to feel this way in such a short amount of time, but truth is ye've had my heart from the start. From the moment ye pulled yerself out of that muddy puddle and gave me a good tongue-lashing."

When he laughed, she smiled and smacked his chest playfully, her heart's beat tripping over itself. "I guess it's a good thing you drive like a maniac."

The uncertainty she'd felt between them melted away in his kisses and in his words. She could lose herself in him for an eternity, but he soon pulled away and the look in his eyes had her uncertainty returning.

"If we're going to be serious about each other, then there's something I need to tell ye, love. It's about Malcolm... and the Hope." He let out a weary sigh. "My brother's an irresponsible arse and unfortunately he managed to involve others in his mess this time around. He thought he had a sure thing going, but didn't have the funds—until he convinced my father to turn over all his savings. Of course, it all failed miserably, and now he needs more funds to try and recoup the money my father gave him, and more than likely to save himself from a severe beating."

It all made sense now. "That's what you were arguing about when we dropped your father off in Edinburgh."

"Aye. My father doesn't know, and I want to keep him from it for as long as I can, since he'd do nothing but worry." His jaw tightened in anger as he ran a rough hand through his hair in frustration. "All my funds are tied up in other ventures, and the banks won't touch this house with the current real estate market."

The pieces fell into place, leaving her gut knotted with dread. "You want to find the necklace so you can use it as collateral."

She got to her feet, desperate to get away from him, her breath coming in shallow gasps, leaving her dizzy. Tears stung her eyes as she tried to work through his betrayal. "You said you wouldn't sell it. I trusted you, Iain."

"I'm not going to sell it, Cat." He grabbed her arm, preventing her from leaving and forcing her to turn and face him. "It would just be on paper as a guarantee until I could free up my funds."

"And if you couldn't come up with the money in time? What then?" She saw the guilt and uncertainty wash over his face and had all the answers she needed. "I'm so glad that being a highlander and a Scot had so much influence in your decision. Or was that just another line you fed me to keep me from your true motives?"

"It's not like that, love, and ye know it." He'd yet to let go of her, which only heightened her emotions.

"Let go of me, Iain." She tried to get her arm free, but his grip was like iron.

"Not until ye hear me out." Iain slowly loosened his hold as if testing to see if she'd run. When she didn't, his shoulders relaxed a bit. "Please sit so I can explain."

"I can't. Not right now." She felt like she couldn't breathe. "I need a bit of space to think and I can't do that here. I'm going back to the inn."

He let out a sigh. "Will ye be gone long?"

She shook her head, but didn't look at him. She couldn't, or he'd weaken her defenses. "I'll probably come back tomorrow, but I'll call to let you know. I just need a little bit of time to clear my head."

"Cat, please don't go." He gave her a hand squeeze, but she slowly pulled away.

"Goodbye, Iain."

She fought back tears and feelings of betrayal all the way to the inn, where she was lucky enough to find they still had a room available, and unlucky enough to run into James.

"Go away, James." She hoisted her bag onto her shoulder and started to go around him, when he grabbed her arm. She glared at him. "Unless you want to lose a hand, I suggest you let me go."

"Trouble in paradise, my dear? You know I'd be happy to cheer you up."

His smile made her want to punch him. "Have you lost your mind, James? Not if you were the last thing with a pulse."

She started to move towards the stairs when his words stopped her. "So you don't want to talk about the Highlander's Hope? I could help, you know."

"Help yourself to the fame and credit is more like it." She shook her head, gritting her teeth. "How the hell did you find out about it? Given that you're a rat, it really shouldn't surprise me, but I want to know what underhanded tactics you used this time around."

"I'm a historian, Catriona. I followed the clues just you like did." He let out a sigh, looking at her as if she were a petulant child. "I just want to help you find the necklace. The sharks are circling, my dear, and you have little time left. We work well together—or have you rewritten your memories so as to not have to face the truth?"

"The truth is that you're a lying bastard and only as good a historian as your thieving skills. And I swear, James, if I find you snooping through my things—here or in Cambridge—I'll make sure you pay for it."

She felt like she couldn't breathe, and every muscle in her body was knotted tight with anger. Why he wouldn't just go away, was beyond her.

"Well, you may have the eldest MacCraigh, but I've got the youngest, and if you're not willing to work together, then I say it's a race to the finish." He laughed at her with his highbrow thin giggle. "Or you could just go home, for I do think, my dear, I have this in the bag."

"We'll just see about that." Without another look, she turned around and headed back out the main door and into the cold.

CHAPTER

Sixteen

I AIN THREW BACK his whisky and wondered how things had gotten so out of hand, how they'd gone so wrong. Duncan leaned his head on the sofa and gave him sad eyes, as if asking him why Cat had to go.

"She'll be back." He took a deep breath and let it out slowly. "Quit giving me that look, dog. I'm none too happy about it either."

The paintings and journals sat there across from him, just the way she'd left them, as if taunting him, a reminder that she was gone. If he couldn't fix things between them, if she couldn't forgive him, he now realized it would leave him devastated.

And for what? All to bail out his brother, who would likely turn around in another year's time and get himself into yet another mess. Of course, it wasn't just his brother. No. Malcolm had made sure to involve his father so there was more at stake than just his sorry arse. It was no wonder his sister had fled at the first opportunity.

It was one day. Come tomorrow, Cat would be back and they would sort things out. And if they didn't? Well it was her loss, wasn't it? There were plenty of women out there, and more than a few who'd be happy to distract him.

And yet... they weren't Cat, were they?

Damn it to hell.

Knowing it would do no good to spend the evening sulking over her, Iain dragged out his laptop and got to work. Grant was taking care of most matters, but there was still plenty to do, most of it woefully neglected.

He shot off a handful of emails, and started to review some files when a knock at the door had Duncan skittering across the room and barking up a storm, his tail wagging. Iain groaned. The last thing he wanted to deal with was his brother—or Nationalists. Grabbing the shotgun, he yanked the door open and found Cat on his front step.

His stomach flipped at the sight of her.

"What happened? Are ye all right?" He stepped to the side so she could come in, and set his weapon down on the sideboard by the door. Something must be wrong for her to not even flinch at being greeted with a gun.

"No. I'm not. Between you and James, I can honestly say I'm having a real shitty day." Her entire body looked stiff, and there was a definite wobble to her voice. "And this does *not* mean I've forgiven you."

"Aye, love. Come have a seat by the fire, and I'll get ye a whisky." With a gentle hand on her back he led her to the library, where she took a seat while he got her a drink.

She'd been upset when she'd left him, and it was doubtful running into James did anything to improve her mood—especially not if it was bad enough to land her back on his doorstep. Making matters worse was that James was now working with his brother, a link back to the reason she was upset with him to begin with.

He sat across from her and leaned forward with his elbows on his knees. "Do ye want to talk about it?"

"Am I stupid?" She looked at him as if it were an earnest question. "Do I have *idiot* tattooed across my forehead?"

He shook his head, dumbfounded. "Cat, ye're one of the smartest women I know. I don't understand what you're asking me."

"Why is it people think they can lie straight to my face? And it's not like it's a one-off, yeah? It happens time and again, and I'm totally clueless."

When she looked away from him with hurt in her eyes, his heart broke to think he was part of the reason she doubted herself. "Cat, I'm sorry. I really am. I was only trying to do right by my family. The men my brother owes money to aren't exactly nice blokes, and though I should let my brother learn from his mistakes, he's dragged my father into it, and I can't let anything happen to him."

She sighed. "Of course not. I'd be devastated to have your father come to harm."

"Unfortunately my options are limited, and the necklace... it was the only thing I could think of to bail my family out of this mess."

She let out a weary sigh, tears of frustration now spilling over. "Is there anything else you're not telling me? Cause I swear, Iain, I won't forgive you if I find out there's more."

"There's nothing else, love." Needing her to believe him, he took her hand in his. "I swear it on my mother's grave."

"There has to be a way to pull together the money, even if the banks won't touch the house. How much does he owe?"

"Too much—over a million, with the interest growing daily."

She made a choking sound. "Bloody hell, Iain."

"Aye. Now ye know." What a mess. The smartest thing she could do would be to run as far as she could from him and this place. "I'm sorry I kept it from ye, but it was also the reason I needed to tell ye, if we were going to pursue something more serious. I still want that for us, Cat, if ye can find it in yer heart to forgive me."

He looked at her in question, wondering whether he'd mucked things up beyond repair.

"I don't know if I can, Iain. I like you, and I like your father. And I get that you're only trying to protect your family. But I don't know if we can just pick up where we left off when it was probably a mistake for me to get involved with you in the first place."

It felt like his heart was breaking. "So I was a mistake?"

"You don't think so?" She scoffed, but he could see the pain in her eyes. "Then you're only kidding yourself. I'd give you a month's time before you grew tired and bored, and found someone new to entertain you."

"Well thank ye kindly for reminding me of what a bastard I am." Didn't she see that the man he was had ceased to exist when he fell for her? "Ye're being unfair, Cat. But I think ye already know that. Don't ye?"

She shrugged, looking indifferent. "Maybe I do. But if you think it changes anything between us, I can tell you that it doesn't. It was a mistake for me to fall for you, and to lose sight that I'm here for only one reason, and that's to find the Highlander's Hope."

"So that's it, then? I tried to be honest with ye, Cat. Does that not count for something?"

"Iain… I don't know what you want me to say. I get why you did it, but I don't know that it changes anything. I'd love to just forget all about this mess, but I don't feel that I can trust you. Maybe if we had time to start fresh, but we don't. I'll be gone as soon as we find the necklace."

He brushed her cheek, unable to stay away when she'd just given him a glimmer of hope. He'd make her see he was worth her trust. "It could take a while to find the necklace. We might end up with plenty of time to try and make this work."

"No, we won't, Iain. I'll have to head back to Cambridge before long, whether we find the necklace or not."

"Then give me what little time we have to convince ye that I'm worth yer trust." With her just a breath away, he nuzzled her cheek, his heart racing when she leaned in to him in response. "Please, Cat. I couldn't bear to leave things between us the way they currently are."

She let out a weary sigh, pulling away enough to look at him. "We can work together to find the Hope, and you can try to change my mind while I'm here, but that's it, Iain. We're not just going to pick up where we left off."

It was all the hope and encouragement he needed, his heart alight as he realized exactly what she meant to him. He ran a hand down her cheek and gave her a quick peck. "As ye wish."

With a finger on his chest, she pushed him away. "No kisses, no hugs, no nibbles, no cuddles. Do you hear me, Iain? We're here to look for the Hope."

His lips quirked into a smile, as his eyes took her in and he resisted the urge to devour her. "Aye, love. I promise to be on my best behavior."

Iain set aside the letters and got up to stretch. Since it was too dark to search the tunnels, they were back to looking at the letters, journals and paintings, but they'd been at it for hours, and he could take little more. "I don't know how ye do it, love. My brain feels like it's turned to mush."

"I'm used to it." She barely looked up from what she was reading.

He'd had enough. Pulling the letters from her hands, he set them aside and hauled her to her feet, ignoring her protests. "Come on. I need to get out of this house or I'm going to go mad."

"And go where? It's late, and we have work to do."

"It can wait." After what happened between them, he had to make it up to her. "I want to show ye something."

"This better be good, Iain." He could see her struggling, trying to keep her distance, despite the smile that tugged at her lips.

From what he knew of her, she just couldn't stay angry or annoyed. Her temper seemed to flair and burn out, a smile and contagious enthusiasm waiting in the wings for the moment when she let down her guard and got tired of being angry. That said, he had no doubt she could truly get mad and hold a grudge—and he pitied the person who pushed her to that extreme. He had no doubt that, if someone made her that angry, it would not fade, and there would be hell to pay. James was a perfect example of that.

"It doesn't often happen, but the Northern Lights can be seen just north of here as of late, and for once, it's a clear night. I thought ye might like to see them." With the promise of a spectacular light show, all put on by Mother Nature, how could she possibly say no? He took her hand and brought it to his lips, his eyes on hers as he waited for her answer.

She bit her lip and continued to debate, but the fact that she hadn't denied him outright gave him hope. "Only if you promise to behave yourself."

"Och, aye. I wouldn't dream of misbehaving."

It was about an hour drive, which ended up feeling like an eternity to Iain. As if to guarantee there would be no chance for romance, Cat had insisted they bring Duncan along for the drive, and in his excitement, he'd been a constant nuisance with his excessive energy, drool and hair. Matters were only made worse by Cat, who barely spoke a word to him, lost in her own thoughts and not willing to share no matter how many times he tried to start a conversation.

They pulled off the road and found a place to park. "Can ye see them, love?"

She leaned forward to look out the windshield and up at the sky. "Oh, Iain, it's beautiful."

"Come on then. I've got a blanket or two in the car boot." He grabbed two blankets and a flashlight, and then led the way through the heather and brush. "Just watch yer step. Ye can take my arm if ye need."

When he offered it to her, she took him up on his offer. "How is it you're so surefooted on such uneven terrain?"

He let out a laugh. "I'm a highlander, love. Been walking these sorts of hills since I was a wee laddie."

They wandered towards the cliffs and sea with Duncan romping at their side. When they found a small clearing, Iain laid out the blanket. The sound of the waves could be heard breaking on the rocks, the perfect accompaniment to the show playing out above them and lighting the sky. He waited for her to get comfortable on the blanket and then took a seat next to her.

"I've got another blanket if ye get cold." They were sliding into November, and the temperatures at night weren't ideal for long periods of time spent exposed to the elements, especially when the wind picked up coming off the water. When she nodded, he spread the blanket over them.

The sky above held her attention as she spoke. "I can't believe it. It's breathtaking, Iain. I didn't realize the Northern Lights made it this far south or that they'd be this bright."

"It's the solar storms we've been having. They've increased the intensity of the lights."

Streaks of aqua and red shimmered across the sky and up to the heavens. They said nothing for a long while, the moment already perfect and not needing words. Even Duncan finally mellowed, now curled up by their feet.

Cat reached out and took his hand in hers, giving it a squeeze as his pulse quickened. "Thank you for bringing me here, Iain. I'll never forget it."

"Aye, love. Neither will I."

When she leaned her head on his shoulder, he wrapped his arm around her and held her close. She let out a sigh, but didn't pull away. "You know this means nothing, right."

"Of course not. As a matter of fact, it ne'er happened."

"Neither did this." She turned towards him and kissed his cheek.

A knot of tension in his shoulders slipped free with the thought that not all hope was lost. He didn't want things to end before they'd given them a fair go, but he also needed to respect her wishes. He'd have to show her she could trust him, and from there, she'd have to take the lead—not that it had been a problem in the past. She was by far the most forthright woman he'd met, and he liked that. A lot.

They'd been quiet for a long while, just taking in the lights, when Cat broke the silence. "What will you do if we don't find the necklace?"

It was a question he wished he had the answer to. "I have no idea. I haven't told my father or sister, knowing they'd do nothing but worry. I'm trying to free up funds. I just don't know if I can manage it in time."

"And if you don't come up with the money? What will they do, Iain?" He could hear the worry in her voice, mirroring the way he felt.

"I don't know, love. I've ne'er dealt with these sorts of people, but I have to take their threats seriously since they involve my brother's well-being. There are days when I'm tempted to let him get his due. Maybe he'll finally learn a lesson. But I couldn't live with myself if he was seriously hurt, and it'd kill my Da." He let out a weary sigh, feeling overwhelmed by the whole thing once again. If there was a clear solution to his problems, he wasn't seeing it.

"But you *do* think that with a bit of time, you could free up enough funds?"

"Aye, love. I'm already moving some of my holdings in that direction, but these things take time, and the bastards my brother's dealing with aren't exactly the patient sort."

She didn't say anything more, but Iain hoped she now saw that his options were limited, and finding the jewels could be the life-line he needed. He'd not risk putting the necklace up as collateral otherwise.

Not yet ready to go, he carefully lay back to watch the sky some more, his head propped on his arms, and his bruises easy to ignore when Cat was so close. "Let me know if ye get cold or want to head back."

"It *is* cold, which is why I'm going to steal some of your heat." She settled back on the blanket and snuggled up against his side, her head nestled against his shoulder as he held her close. "Do I need to say it?"

"Say what? That this ne'er happened?" He laughed and kissed the top of her head. "It's already forgotten, love."

"Good. Then you won't remember any of this either—which is not to say you're off the hook. Yeah?" Cat brushed her thumb across his lips, and then kissed him with complete abandon.

He lost himself in the nearness of her, in her touch, in her kisses, his heart aching with the want of her. He gave her all he had, including his very soul, there under the brilliance of sky and stars, as they came together as one.

Come morning, Duncan's distant barks rang in Iain's ears, pulling him from his slumber. He awoke to find Cat in his arms and in his bed, still not quite believing the night they'd had. In the short time he'd known her, she'd turned his world upside down, and he didn't know if it'd ever get put right again—not that he wanted it to. The relationships he'd had in the past seemed like a distant memory and a pale comparison to what he had with Cat.

"Come on, love. Wake up. We've got a necklace to find, and Angus will be knocking on our door and giving us looks." He gave her a kiss as she started to stir.

She popped one sleepy eye open and looked at him. "Oh, crap. How the hell did this happen? *You...* you snuck in past my defenses with freezing temperatures and celestial light shows."

"And a good morning to ye, too." He laughed, knowing better than to take offense. Whatever relationship they did have, it defied definition and convention. "How's breakfast sound?"

With her grunt of agreement, he threw on something comfortable and headed out to find the dog, that was, no doubt, desperate to go out. Despite the troubles looming over his head, Iain found himself in a damned good mood.

He ground some coffee beans and got a pot going, the deep rich scent filling the air as it started to brew. After the night they'd had, there was a good chance Cat would be hungry once she got around to waking up. With a loud rumble, his stomach reminded him that she wasn't the only one in need of nourishment.

Iain was half way through frying some black pudding, rashers and eggs, when Cat wandered into the kitchen and wrapped her arms around his waist from behind, leaning her head against his back.

"What are ye doing up? I thought ye'd sleep until noon—or at the very least until I woke ye up with breakfast in bed." Damn if it wasn't hard to concentrate on the task at hand, when his body's response to having her close was automatic.

"I could smell the coffee all the way up on the second floor. Impossible to sleep through it."

Iain could hear the smile in her voice. "Do me a favor and drop some toast?"

"Sure." She went up on her toes and nipped at his ear, the absence of her touch already missed as she moved over to the toaster. "Seems like you do a lot of cooking."

"Aye. It's just me and my Da now, so I primarily take care of it." He flipped the eggs for just a second, and then transferred the food to the plates he'd heated in the Aga. "My mother used to do most of the cooking."

"Your dad mentioned her." She looked over at him, worried. "I'm sorry. I can't imagine."

"It's been a few years, and it gets easier with time." He changed the subject, not wanting to think about how his mother would have adored her. "Angus will be here in the next hour or so—earlier if he catches wind of food."

Iain got a good look at her, and what he saw made his heart catch. By the gods she was gorgeous with the remnants of sleep clinging to her. Wearing on oversized sweatshirt with a scoop neck cut out of it, it hung precariously over a bare shoulder. She'd paired it with thermals that showed off shapely legs and rag wool socks. She looked casually delicious, especially with her dark curls misbehaving as they escaped the braid trying to tame them.

"I like Angus." She put a few buttered slices of toast on each plate and then carried them to the table.

"Most women do. How he's managed to stay single while at the same time having women fawn all over him is beyond me." Despite the night they'd had, he looked over at her to see if she too had fallen victim to his friend's charms. What he saw gave him hope.

"He seems awfully sweet." She gave him a smile and a shrug. "But I think I'm glad you're the one who nearly ran me over. It must have been your grand scheme from the very start, ensuring that I fell... for your charms."

Was she going to say something different? And why didn't she? Didn't she know how he felt about her? Yet he had to laugh at himself, when he'd yet to admit to himself what she meant to him.

So he took that step, even if it was in the silence of his own head.

He loved her. Utterly and completely.

CHAPTER
Seventeen

C AT FOLLOWED BEHIND Angus with Iain taking the rear, the trail too narrow to accommodate them all at once. The solitude of their surroundings and the fresh air were exactly what she needed to clear her head and ground herself.

She had no problem with the occasional casual fling—not that she got much opportunity with her nose constantly buried in a book—but she'd let this go far beyond casual. Even with her pulling back after Iain's confession, she'd been unable to remain angry with him, still craving his touch and his company. It was hard for her to ignore the way she felt about him, even if she should be keeping him at arm's length.

She'd just have to hold her ground and not give in. After all, she'd done *such* an amazing job of it up until now. Sarcasm aside, she knew he could tear her heart to pieces if this didn't work out, and the odds were against them. He lived and worked in the highlands, and led a glamorous life with parties and the famous, whereas she was in Cambridge and hadn't worn a pair of heels since her brother's wedding.

Her heart told her he seemed comfortable living a quiet life, and she could certainly lose herself in the history of the surrounding area, but it was her mind that kept weighing the facts and telling her she'd be a fool.

"We're nearly there." Angus looked back over his shoulder with a smile, his blue eyes alight with intelligence and humor.

She had to wonder if Angus picked up on her internal conflict about Iain. It would seem the man missed nothing.

Best to keep her mind off Iain then. "It's so beautiful here. I'd love to spend some time exploring once this is over." She took a deep breath, her lungs filling with the scents of pine and heather. She'd be sorry to leave this place when the time came—and it'd be even harder to leave Iain.

Damn it if her heart wasn't kicking her mind's ass.

Iain stepped to her side as the path opened up a bit, matching his pace to hers. "Does that mean ye'll stay a wee bit longer?"

"It's hard to say. I've got my studies and grad students to get back to, and I'll have used up my free time if we don't find the Hope soon." Though there was disappointment in his eyes, it looked like he might also take it as a challenge—and she might very well enjoy him trying to convince her to stay.

"There's the tree. And we're not far from the Bleeding Heart, aye?" Iain tilted his head towards a large oak, the branches of it splayed in an odd configuration. The lower branches pointed down towards the earth, whereas the upper ones tangled together, stretching upwards. Just like in the painting. "Look just behind it, at the stony outcropping."

A craggy cliff face jutted up out of the ground, sparse with greenery. Cat searched the stony wall from where they stood, but didn't see any openings. "Do you think there could be another cave?"

Squinting to focus, Iain looked past the tree as if searching the shadows. "Aye, love. Let's take a closer look."

Standing at the bottom of the cliff, it was still hard to see any openings. Yet despite all the obstacles, Cat's heart raced with anticipation and the hope they might be close to finding the necklace.

Angus pointed. "There. Is that something? Or am I seeing things?"

The area was partially hidden by brush, the leaves gone for winter. It was hard to tell whether or not there was anything there from where they stood, but the texture and shading seemed slightly different. Better yet, it wouldn't be noticeable unless you were looking for it, making it all the more likely that it might have been used to hide the jewels.

"Aye, I think it might be. Let's have a look." Iain gave her hand a squeeze. "It's a bit steep. Do ye think ye can manage it or would ye rather wait here until we know more?"

She laughed. "You are kidding, right?"

He shrugged with a smile. "Just thought I'd ask—not that I expected ye to stay here waiting."

They started the upwards climb, the path all but disappearing in places, so they were forced to grab hold of shrubbery. Iain lent a steadying hand where needed, and truth was she was happy for his help, especially the higher up they got.

Having taken the lead, Angus looked over at them with a smile and then disappeared into the cliff side. Excitement overtook fear, and along with Iain's help, Cat managed to not go crashing to the ground below, but was instead pulled into the opening by Angus, with Iain following just behind her.

When she looked out the hole to the drop below, it left her so dizzy, she was forced to take a step back to clear her head. "I sure as hell hope there's another way out of here, because I can tell you now, there's no way I'm making it back down unless I suddenly sprout hooves and horns, and magic myself into a billy goat."

Angus laughed. "It's always easier to go up than to go down, and even easier to crack yer head open like an egg."

"Ye always know how to put a girl at ease." Iain smirked at his friend, and then, ignoring Angus's shit-eating grin, he pulled the flashlights out of his pack along with some heavy twine. "Just in case the tunnel branches off. I'd rather not get lost if I can help it."

Angus flashed his light around, and took a few steps towards the darkness. "Looks like it continues."

"Aye, let's get started then." Iain found a branch at the entrance and anchored the twine to it. Grabbing his flashlight, he hoisted his backpack over a shoulder. "After you."

Cat noticed how the two of them always kept her in the middle, like a pair of floppy-eared sheepdogs watching a lone sheep. It was sweet of them, and even sweeter that they'd come about it without discussion, their protective nature automatically leading them. Then she thought of the necklace and why Iain had thought of using it as collateral, and it made even more sense. It was his nature to try and take care of the people around him. It didn't mean he'd been right to lie to her, but she understood why. The people he loved came first above all else.

Iain handed her a flashlight. "Just in case ye need it."

Wandering behind Angus, she was happy he'd taken the lead. The amount of cobwebs he was sweeping to the side made her hair stand on end. No doubt she'd spend the next week trying to ignore the feeling that bugs were crawling all over her. Ten minutes in, the tunnel forked.

"Left or right?" Angus turned to them in question.

Iain stepped past her to give the tunnels a quick examination. "I don't think it'll matter either way. May as well start with the left and then back-track to search the right."

The tunnel continued for some time, the air damp and cold, laden with the scent of the earth. And then it continued some more.

"This seems to be one long tunnel. I can't imagine it's completely natural." Maybe part of it had been, but Cat suspected a good portion of it was extended over the centuries.

"It's not unusual to get some pretty long tunnels this close to the ocean, but this one's had more than a little help, especially if it ends up where I suspect it might." Iain moved up to her side. "With the direction we've been heading, I think we may very well end up back at the house—or not far from it."

"It would make sense since we know they were likely housing Jacobites." Cat thought of the hidden room they'd found when MacTavish showed up. Though it would make sense to keep the jewels hidden someplace close like these tunnels, they may not want them directly linked to the house. There'd be too great a chance the English might find the tunnel while looking for Jacobites—and then find the jewels. "They may not want the tunnel linked directly to the house, though, especially if the necklace is hidden here."

Iain nodded. "Aye. I see what you're getting at. There'd be less chance of finding the openings to the tunnels."

They followed the tunnel to the end, peeking out the narrow opening to get their bearings. Of course, Cat hadn't the foggiest of clues as to where they were.

With an arm around her waist, Iain came up from behind her, making her forget she was likely covered in cobwebs. "We're not far, love. The house is just over the hill there. Are ye up for heading back to check out the other tunnel?"

"I am, if you guys are up for it." She pulled a water bottle from her backpack and took a long drink, the others following suit. "James is still sniffing around, and I want the necklace found. I can't let it fall into his hands."

Angus sighed. "He seems to like causing trouble. Was he always such an arse?"

"You mean, why the hell did I date him?" Cat had to laugh. How many times had she asked herself that same question? "James is good at masking his true nature—for a little while, anyway. Luckily, I learned my lesson the first time around, and it'll be a cold day in hell before I fall for him again, try as he might."

She felt Iain stiffen at her side. "And has he been trying?"

"I've been quick enough to put an end to his nonsense, and it's not like it was ever anything more than a way to get to the necklace or my research. He's never cared about anyone but himself." Cat didn't want to think about the mistakes she'd made. She felt like an idiot for having fallen for James in the first place—and the last thing she wanted to do was discuss her stupidity and her prior relationships. "Can we go? I want to make sure we finish searching this tunnel, and try to find any others by the Bleeding Heart."

"Angus, could you give us a moment? We'll catch up." Once Angus had gone, Iain took her hands in his. "Cat, ye can't give James a second thought. I know it bothers ye that ye trusted him when he didn't deserve it, but it's in the past. Dinnae fash yerself, love. There isn't a person alive who hasn't made that sort of mistake."

She felt weary, but his words did help. Sliding her arms around his waist, she leaned her head against his chest, the pounding of his heart soothing her. "Are you always this nice?"

He shrugged. "Aye. When I'm not running people over or into ditches."

Laughing, Cat went onto her toes and kissed his cheek. "You're a sweet man, Iain. Now let's go find that necklace."

"As ye wish, love."

"It looks odd, right?" Cat looked at the end of the tunnel, wondering if she was imagining it, the shadows casting things in an odd light.

Having backtracked to where the tunnel split in two, they'd followed the right side this time around, though it wasn't long before the tunnel came to an abrupt end. No rubble or a rough stone wall. Instead it looked... off. Not terribly different from the surrounding walls, but no one would likely notice the difference unless they were really looking.

Cat touched it, rubbing her hands together. "Almost feels like clay mixed with stone."

Iain did the same, as if trying to determine the composition of the wall. "Aye, it does, though I wouldn't say it's unusual. There's a wee bit of clay to be found not far from the loch."

"But it seems like it was formed to look like the tunnel came to an end. Somehow, it just doesn't look completely natural to me." Cat shined her light on the area again, taking a closer look. Maybe it was just wishful thinking on her part. "You guys would know better. I don't exactly get to go crawling through caves and tunnels on a regular basis."

Angus tilted his head in Iain's direction. "And ye think he does? All suits, meetings, and corporate takeovers. He hasn't been climbing through these tunnels since he was a lad."

Dropping his backpack on the ground, Angus started rooting around in it and pulled out a small folded camping shovel, as half of the other contents in the bag spilled out in the process.

Cat had to laugh. "Bloody hell, how much stuff do you have crammed in there? It must be like the Tardis—bigger on the inside."

"A Doctor Who fan?" Iain's voice was laced with humor. "*Who* knew?"

"*Who*, indeed." Angus chimed in with a laugh.

Cat gave the two men a warm smile. "Have to say—there's nothing I like more in a handsome man than a touch of geek. Even better when there are two of them."

"Och, we're happy to oblige ye, lass." Angus folded back the handle of the shovel and clicked it into place as he stood. "Shall we have a go, then?"

The way he held the shovel, there was no doubt in Cat's mind what he intended to do with it. Iain pulled her back. "He's dangerous with this sort of thing. Nearly took my head off when we were kids."

The thwack of metal against the solid wall left Cat cringing, the sound bouncing off the walls. Angus hit the wall again and again with the point of the shovel, pausing occasionally to check on his progress.

"Ye know, if it's solid, ye'll be digging awhile."

"Well, if ye'd been as well prepared as I am, ye could help. I mean who comes on a treasure hunt without a shovel?" There was a teasing humor in Angus's voice as he ribbed his friend. "I guess I'll have to go it alone, though ye can pay me back with a nice pint."

"Just the one?"

"Och, well, if ye insist, ye could make it two or three—and a bite to eat wouldn't go amiss, either." Another blow at the wall. "I'm working up a thirst and an appetite here."

The sincere friendship between Angus and Iain set Cat at ease, making her like the two of them even more. Not that Iain hadn't already managed to finagle his way back into her good graces. He had a knack for that, it'd seem.

"Would ye look at that." Angus put down the shovel and ran his hand over the wall.

Iain stepped forward with his flashlight, shinning it onto the ragged hole Angus had managed to create. Giving her a smile over his shoulder, he said, "Ye were right, love. Looks like there might be something behind there."

Cat's excitement could be barely be contained, racing through her like a lightning storm. Experience told her it would likely be nothing—or perhaps they'd find another clue—yet she couldn't help but be hopeful. All the signs they'd found kept leading them to the lands surrounding the MacCraigh home, and this tunnel seemed as good a place as any to hide the necklace.

Angus turned to Iain who was trying to peek through the small hole. "Step back so I can widen the hole. Don't want ye getting in the way. Liable to get yer eye poked out, and I'd be the one to blame." With the shovel raised and at the ready, Angus patiently waited until Iain was out of the way.

"Ah yes, because it wouldn't be yer fault when ye're the one swinging a camping shovel like ye're Thor." Though Iain teased his friend, he still got out of the way; also taking the time to make sure Cat was at a safe distance. To Cat he said, "I couldn't see much, but it looks like there's something back there. There were iron bars, love. Someone's gone to an awful lot of trouble to keep people out."

She leapt at him with her arms wrapped around his neck as he held onto her and gave her a kiss. "Even if it turns out to be nothing, it makes me optimistic that it's only a matter of time before we find it."

"Aye, love. We'll find it before long." His voice trailed off towards uncertainty, and she knew it was because she'd be leaving once they found the Hope.

Though she couldn't tell him she'd stay, she gave his a hand a squeeze and then leaned into him, her lips lingering on his in a slow, sweet kiss. Knowing it'd be too easy to keep kissing him, she forced herself to put some distance between them.

"I should take some pictures for my research paper." She pulled her pack off and gently lowered it to the ground so she could dig out her camera. There was a decent flash on it, so hopefully it'd do. "Let me know when you're ready, Angus."

"Look at that, would ye?" Angus stepped back out of the way, wiping an arm across his forehead. The hole was a foot and a half wide and close to three feet long.

"Here, let me get ye a bit of light." Iain stepped to the side so the beam would fall where Cat needed it, but he wouldn't get in her way while she took her pictures.

Cat pulled off the lens cap and immediately started clicking away, taking only enough time to make sure her pictures were focused. She stepped closer, her heart racing as adrenaline pumped through veins.

"The bars are just beyond the clay wall and look rusted in places." Cat reached in and gave them a shake. "They're still holding though. Give me a flashlight?"

"Here ye are, lass." Angus handed her his.

She shone it into the hole, her pulse tripping over itself. A dozen or so large wooden boxes lay piled one on top of the other, filling the small space. "Well, I'll be damned."

CHAPTER
Eighteen

"UNLESS YE KNOW how to pick a lock, we'll have to come back tomorrow with some bolt cutters. It's too late to do it tonight." Iain saw the disappointment in Cat's eyes, but there was nothing for it. "We'll come back first thing, since we'd not make it to the house and back before dark."

"What about the other branch of the tunnel?" There'd been yet another fork. "I'd still like to see where it leads."

"Tomorrow, love. We'll not manage the difficult terrain once the sun sets."

Angus came to his aid. "He's right, lass. A hike in the dark would only result in sprained or broken limbs, and despite my Tardis-like rucksack, I have no camping equipment with me."

Cat let out a weary sigh and managed a smile. "I know. It's just that we're *so* close, even if this ends up being nothing more than provisions or someone's secret stash of chocolate-covered Hobnobs."

"Given my sister's predilection for the chocolate treats, ye may very well be right." Iain ran a hand down her arm. "We'll be back at sun-up. We got a lot accomplished, and we're one step closer, love."

She nodded, and with a final glance over her shoulder at what could be the find of a lifetime, they headed home.

With Angus offering to host dinner for the night, Iain drove over with Cat nestled in the seat beside him. "It's just up ahead. I think ye'll like his place. He's been renovating it for the last few years now."

As they turned down a long drive, the house came into view, the lights left on for them. "It was once a hunting lodge that had fallen into disrepair, and before that, a small manor. Angus has had a wee bit of help, but surprisingly enough, has done a fair amount of the work himself."

"It's gorgeous, Iain. I adore the stone walls and the way the wooden beams jut out from under the roofline." She gave his hand a squeeze. "So many windows too. Must be nice on a sunny day."

"Aye, it is. And ye can't tell since it's dark, but the sea lies just beyond. The view's incredible." He parked the car before shifting in his seat to face her.

Brushing the hair from her face, he let his touch linger. What the hell had happened to him? Why was it he couldn't bear to let her go? It got him thinking. Perhaps that was exactly what he needed to do. Maybe if she realized it would soon be over, she'd think twice about actually going. "I just wanted to tell ye that I've enjoyed our time together. I know ye've got to get back once we find the Hope, but I do hope ye'll not sever all ties."

"No... of course not." She looked away, unease and worry tainting her voice.

Though Iain wanted to reassure her, he couldn't. It was her decision to make, but if she was going to walk away, then he wasn't going to make it easy for her. He'd just have to make her realize what it would be like if they weren't in each other's lives.

"I'm glad to hear it then. Maybe if ye have time off from yer research next summer we could get together. Catch up on what ye been doing. Grab some dinner."

"Summer? That's seven months away." Another sigh as she looked away. "I suppose you'll be busy catching up on business and sorting out your brother's problems once I'm gone."

"Aye. Grant's been hounding me with emails, and though he's capable of dealing with things, there are still matters I need to tend to. With that said, I wouldn't give up the time we've had together for anything." He brushed her cheek with the back of his hand. "I'm going to miss ye, Cat."

"And I'll miss you."

When she leaned in and kissed him, his heart thundered away at the possibilities—or what could be lost. With their heads bowed together, their cheeks touching, Iain took a moment to hold onto what time they had together before forcing himself to let her go. "We should go in. Angus will be cooking up a storm."

He started to go, but she put a hand on his arm. "Wait, Iain."

Turning back towards her, he tried not to sound too hopeful. "What is it, love?"

"Maybe… I don't know." She shrugged and looked like she was mulling things over in that pretty head of hers. "Maybe you could come down to Cambridge during spring break and we could spend the week together."

"A week? Cat, what's the point in prolonging the inevitable? Ye don't want to pursue anything serious, and I like ye too much to keep this casual." He let out a weary sigh. Why couldn't she just tell him she'd stay? "I've yet to earn back enough of yer trust for ye to consider staying, and it's only a matter of time before we find the Hope and ye leave."

The silence drew out between them, as he waited for her response. Finally, she shook her head. "It wasn't supposed to happen like this, Iain. None of it."

"Well it did. Now what are ye going to do about it?" Frustration had his muscles in knots. "The decision is yers to make, Cat. But I'll not be waiting around forever. Life goes on, and I know better than to let it pass me by. Ye can't let the past keep ye from living in the present."

"I know that, Iain."

"Do ye? 'Cause I'm not so sure." Annoyed, he didn't want to say something he'd regret. "Come on. Angus is waiting."

"I don't know what you want me from, Iain."

"I want ye to stop ignoring how ye feel. What's between us is more than just sex, Cat, and ye'd be lying if ye said otherwise." He wanted to shake her until her teeth rattled and she saw sense.

"How I feel about you makes no difference. It doesn't change that you lied to me, or that I have to head back Cambridge—and it certainly doesn't change the fact that our lives are incompatible."

"Are they now? And when did ye decide this, pray tell?" He scoffed. "I'd think having a wealthy benefactor to fund yer research would suit ye just fine. Just think of the expeditions ye could launch."

"And in exchange? What? I sleep with you?" Despite the lack of light, Cat was clearly angry. "Are you implying I should prostitute myself for my research?"

"Of course not. Ye're putting words in my mouth." How did this get so out of control? All he wanted was to make her see sense. "I'm just trying to point out that our lives aren't so incompatible."

"What I meant is that your relationships haven't lasted longer than a month. I'm only going by your own track record, Iain. I'm sorry, but I can't remain detached when it comes to you, and I'd rather not have my heart broken."

"Is it because ye're in love with me?" He cursed himself for asking, and yet he waited without taking a breath, his heart all but stopping. "Why can't ye just admit it?"

"Why should I? It's not like you have."

He burst out laughing, the weight on his chest lifting just a little. She hadn't denied it. And that was all he needed for now. "I do love ye, Cat. Gods help me, but I do. Don't even know how it happened. But it did. And before ye go saying anything, don't. I know ye're not ready, and when ye do tell me ye love me, I want it to be because ye mean it and it's something ye're comfortable with."

It looked like she was still mulling over his words—mulling over the fact that he'd declared his love her. When she spoke, she sounded short of breath, her next words nothing more than a pawn moved in the game they were playing. "You're awfully sure of yourself, MacCraigh."

He had to smile. "Aye. Of some things, I am. Now let's get us some dinner. I'm famished."

Without another word, he got out of the car and jogged over to get her door before she had a chance to exit. She took his offered hand but only after she glared at him. Yet despite her best attempts, there was no heat or anger behind it, and it only widened his smile.

"This does *not* mean I'm in love with you, Iain."

"Of course not." Unable to help himself, his smile stretched ear to ear.

Angus answered the door, wiping his hands on a kitchen towel. "Took the two of ye long enough to get here. The food's going cold."

"Ye're like an old biddy when it comes to getting yer food on the table." He clapped his friend on the back and followed him into the kitchen. "What's for dinner?"

"Steak and tatties, caramelized onions and garlic, with a side of sprouts that I pan-fried with bacon." Angus always managed to whip together elaborate meals with ease.

"Ye know, ye make me look bad when all I typically manage are fried eggs."

"Not my fault, is it?" Angus's eyes danced with mischief as they fell into their comfortable routine of teasing each other. "Has the man not been feeding ye, Cat?"

"As a matter of fact, he's kept me well fed." She looked around the kitchen, and Iain could tell she was impressed. Though Angus's home wasn't as large as his own, it certainly had ample room and Angus had done a great job of keeping the old details of the home while updating it with modern touches. "Angus, I won't delay dinner any further, but when we're done eating, you're going to have to give me a tour of this place. It's amazing."

"I'd be glad to."

With a bottle of wine opened and the food served, they sat down to an incredible meal. Conversation was kept light, and Iain was happy to see Cat enjoying herself. And yet... every time her gaze strayed in his direction, he saw a certain unease come over her, making him wonder if he'd pushed her too far, too soon.

Angus pulled him from his thoughts. "Did I tell ye about Rowan? She's a family friend, though I've ne'er met her—she's from the States too. Anyway, she'll be moving here in the next month or two. We've been emailing a lot, since I'm helping her get situated. Going to stay over at the Campbell cottage by the stones. Belongs to her Ma, though she's not been back in decades and Rowan's ne'er come to visit."

"Ah." Iain had heard the stories of Iona Campbell. She'd moved away, pregnant and unwed. Seemed the daughter was now coming back to her roots. But there was more. If Iain had to guess, Angus was smitten with the lass. "So it's Rowan, is it? And will ye be showing her around?"

Cat thwacked him. "Leave the poor man alone. I think it's sweet."

Iain linked his hand with hers and brought it to his lips. "That's because ye're a hopeless romantic, my dear."

She glanced in Angus's direction before turning back to face him, suddenly looking like a fox being chased down by hounds. "No. I'm not. I'm practical, Iain."

Iain thought that if they hadn't been in the middle of a dinner that took Angus so long to prepare, Cat would have bolted then and there. He was losing her again. He did his best to be honest about wanting to use the necklace as collateral and she'd understood, yet she was still skittish about him, and her past hurts were still clouding her judgment. Well, if she thought he'd be fool enough to let her go over her unsubstantiated fears, then she best think again.

They loved each other—of that he had no doubt. He just had to make her see the truth of it.

With his patience thin as spring ice over a lake, he rushed them through the rest of the evening, desperate to get her home so they could sort out the matter once and for all. He ignored Angus's looks of suspicion and Cat's looks of annoyance.

He'd never had so little control over a situation. Not even with his brother's mess. It was driving him to the edge—and Cat was the one responsible for their little rollercoaster ride.

"What about dessert?" Angus immediately started to protest when Iain got to his feet and declared he and Cat would be calling it a night and heading home. "I made a trifle."

"Ye can bring it with ye tomorrow. Ye'll be coming with us back to the tunnel?"

"Aye. I'll see ye first thing in the morning then."

"Cat... would ye hold up?" Iain knew she'd be angry with him for rudely dragging her away in the middle of dinner so they could sort out their problems, but he'd miscalculated her temper just a wee bit. Her silence during the car ride was only the calm before the storm.

"What the hell was that about?" She stormed through the door, the moment he had it opened. Duncan, oblivious to the tension between them, wagged his tail and went after her.

Well, Iain had a temper too, and he'd be damned if he wasn't going to get this sorted out once and for all. "I thought ye'd be wanting to come home and pack. After all, ye'll be high-tailing it out of here as soon as we find the necklace."

She spun on him, fury in her eyes. "You're a jerk. You know that?"

"Och, love. How could I forget it when ye remind me every chance ye get?" Iain scoffed at her with a shake of his head.

Her cheeks flushed red. "I do not. And if the shoe fits…"

"Ye know, ye contradict yerself at every turn. Ye say ye don't call me a jerk, but they're the next words out of yer gob. Ye kiss me and then say it ne'er happened. Ye get angry with me and want to leave, but then take me to yer bed. Well, I've had it, Cat. No more."

"Well, pardon me for making that mistake. And here I thought we were having fun." She shrugged her shoulder with a tilt of her head, as if dismissing him.

"Is that what ye call it? Fun?" The girl left him dizzy. "Listen to me, love. Ye have it so I don't know which end is up anymore."

"How is that my fault, when I'm just falling in line with the life you've led?" She shook her head, her arms crossed in front of her chest, closing her off and putting even more distance between them.

"I'm telling ye that's no longer the case, Cat. Yet ye won't let it go."

The tension in her body seemed to ease a little. "Our lives are too different, Iain, and we're each going in different directions. We want different things."

"Do we? Well, I don't think so, Cat."

"I need a real relationship—and let's face it, you're not the real relationship type. I just don't think you can change, even if there's nothing I want more."

"Is that what ye think? Well, let me prove ye wrong then. Marry me, Cat." His heart was pounding in his ears and it felt like he couldn't breathe, yet at the same time, it felt so perfectly right. He took her hands in his, ignoring the confusion written all over her face. "Cat, I love ye with all my heart and I know ye feel the same about me. Marry me, love."

She pulled her hands free and took a step away from him, anger creasing her brow. "Go away, Iain. You're insane."

"Then be insane with me. Say *yes.*"

Cat shook her head and sent a scathing glare in his direction. "I'm not even going to acknowledge your question with an answer. And you should be ashamed of yourself to be asking something so important with such casualness and disregard, just so you can prove your point."

Iain stepped to her side and wrapped an arm around her waist, ready to devour her with his eyes, his soul. "Trust me when I tell ye, love, I'd not ask ye to marry me if I didn't mean it."

With a hand on his chest she slipped, wiggled and pushed her way out of his arms, as his smile widened, recognizing this as a game they'd played before. "You're insane, Iain."

"Och, I'll not deny this seems a bit mad, but I love ye, Cat." He couldn't help but smile, for he truly did love her, and all her quirky ways. He could already see her defenses melting, for he had no doubt they were meant to be together. "Say yes, love. I promise ye'll not regret it."

As if shaking herself out of a trance, she stepped away from him. "I have to go."

"Go where?" Gone was his smile, now replaced by worry.

"To the inn. I can't do this right now. Most of my things are still packed, but I'll pick up the rest tomorrow."

"It's not safe, Cat, and ye know it. Have ye forgotten about the attack? And ye're not going anywhere until we sort out what's between us." He ran a rough hand through his hair, surely making him look crazed.

She sighed, and shook her head. "I can't marry you, Iain. And trust me—you'll thank me in the long run. You're only going down this road because you see me as a challenge. I haven't acted like the dozens of other women you've dated, so you jump to the conclusion that it must be love. Well, it's not."

"Is that what ye really think?" Didn't she see that she'd changed his entire world—had changed what he wanted from life?

"I need to go. This is going nowhere, and doing neither of us any good. We can't keep having this conversation."

"Only because ye ne'er sit down so we can sort it out. Ye're constantly running scared, lass, and I'm trying to tell ye, ye have nothing to fear— not from me anyway."

"Oh, trust me. I have plenty to fear from you. You're the only one making my life screwy, Iain. I was supposed to come here, find the Hope, write my paper to academic acclaim, and move on to my next project. Falling in love and getting married? Not part of the plan."

She turned to go, but he grabbed her arm and pulled her to him, his lips on hers, taking with wanton abandon, her protests melting in the heat of passion. "Marry me, Cat. I'm going to keep asking ye until ye say yes."

Their lips locked again, as he consumed her with his very soul, no longer needing breath as long as he had her.

Between kisses she managed to get her response out. "I'm ignoring you, Iain MacCraigh. You asking that question? Never happened."

He let out a chuckle against her lips, lifting her off her feet as she wrapped her legs around his waist. "If ye say so, love."

By the time they made it to his room, he could barely string together a coherent thought—except that she had yet to push him away and was returning his passions. With every fiber of his being, he wanted her. With every breath. With every beat of his heart.

And then she pushed him away, her breath coming in heavy as she moved away from him. "I can't do this, Iain."

"Cat, please... don't do this." His heart fell into a slow shatter. "Stay."

She was already heading for the door. "I won't go to the inn, but I can't keep doing this. It's got to stop. Goodnight, Iain."

"As ye wish, love." He let out a ragged sigh laden with hurt and un-fulfilled desire. "As ye wish."

Come morning, Iain awoke to Duncan's incessant barking, a sure sign that Iain's bad mood would only worsen. Pushing Cat from his mind, he followed the commotion to the library and found his brother and James sitting on the sofa across from the paintings. "What the hell are ye doing here? After the shite ye pulled the other night, neither of ye are welcome here."

"It's my home as much as it's yers, Iain." Malcolm stood and faced him, a look of smug arrogance on his face.

"Ye eejit. Yer big mouth had nationalists traipsing through the home with weapons." He fisted his brother's shirt. "They hit Cat over the head hard enough to render her unconscious. So don't go telling me that ye have a right to be here—ye lost that privilege when ye gambled yerself into a hole. Da's left the house to me. Ye have no claim here, Malcolm."

His brother shrugged out of Iain's grasp. "That's where ye'd be wrong. The house is only yers once Da passes, and until then ye've no more claim on it than I. We're here to find the Highlander's Hope, and if ye think ye're going to stop us, then you can guess again."

He tried his best to mask any acknowledgement of the necklace. "Ye're daft. Cat may be a historian, but she's only here for one reason, and that's me. You and yer friends have ruined what was supposed to be a romantic holiday."

James tilted his head towards Cat's laptop, and let out a laugh that made Iain want to punch him. "I know Cat, and trust me when I tell you, the girl is here for the necklace. She is nothing if not meticulous in her documentation, even if she doesn't refer to the Highlander's Hope by name."

"That's password-protected." Iain's temper rose.

"Is it? I hadn't noticed." James laughed, looking smug.

It was a hunch, and Iain went with it, his temper flaring. "Ye've had remote access to her computer, haven't ye? Set it up the last time ye got yer hands on it."

There were plenty of programs out there that allowed external users remote control—and if you didn't know what to look for, you'd never know. All one needed was access to the computer just once to download the program, and James had the opportunity when he and Cat had been dating.

James looked so smug, it made Iain want to plant a fist in his face. "I have no idea what you're talking about, but I'd be careful about making any accusations. I could take you to court for slander."

"Go for it." Furious, Iain would love a fight.

"Is it true, James?" Cat walked into the room, her hair disheveled, and her eyes ablaze as she zeroed in on her ex. She then laughed, shaking her head—but only a fool would take it for humor. "I can't believe it."

When she lunged for James, murder in her eyes, Iain grabbed her with an arm around her waist, trying to keep his grip on her as she struggled to kill the bastard. "He's not worth it, love."

"No, he's not."

Iain spun at the unfamiliar voice, dread filling him at the sight of three armed men, and in the lead, the same nationalist they'd dealt with before. Malcolm must have left the door unlocked—or let them in. "What do ye want? If ye're looking for the Hope, we don't have it, nor did we have it at any point. I don't want trouble."

Putting Cat down, he shifted her behind him to try and keep her safe. He didn't know how serious these men were about using their weapons, but he sure as hell wasn't going to take a chance.

It was his brother who stepped forward. "What the hell are ye doing, MacTavish? Ye were only supposed to help us find the Hope. This was *not* part of the deal."

"We have no deal, MacCraigh, so I suggest ye sit down and shut yer gob." He waved his gun towards them. "The rest of ye, too—except for the lass. She's coming with me."

CHAPTER
Nineteen

"I'LL BE FINE." Cat tried desperately to reassure Iain as one of the men shoved a gun at him. She'd never been more frightened, but knew she needed to keep a level head. If she could find out what they wanted, she might be able to get rid of them.

MacTavish grabbed her arm and pushed her towards the door and out of the room, Iain's shouts fading as they moved down the hall and into the sitting room. MacTavish pushed her into a seat and stood across from her, his gun pointed right at her.

"This is simple, really. I want the necklace, and if ye don't already have it, then you're going to find it. Are we clear?" What *was* clear by his tone was that he was damn serious about finding the Hope.

"Just one problem—it might not even be here. And even if it is, I'm sure it's well hidden. It could take us forever to find it." It was nothing but the truth, even if she felt their recent discovery of the tunnel and hidden chamber could indeed hold the Hope. "Historians and archaeologists spend years looking for these types of finds—lifetimes even—and usually come up empty-handed. What are you going to do? Hold us at gunpoint while we grow old and grey?"

He let out a bark of a laugh. "Nae, lass. I'll have shot all of ye long before that, starting with yer lad. So I suggest ye get a move on. I've no doubt that, properly motivated, ye'll make good use of yer time."

"Trust me when I tell you, he's not my lad or anything more than a pain in my ass." She didn't want MacTavish thinking they could hurt Iain to get to her. It was doubtful it would work, but it was still worth a try.

"That may well be the case, but either way, I don't think ye'd want him bleeding out on the carpet."

"You know, I fully support the Nationalist movement, but you're really starting to tick me off."

He shook his head with a chuckle one would never expect to come from such a man. "Ye've got a bit of fire to ye. I can see why he likes ye. Now let's not ruin things for him by making me shoot one of ye. It'd be a pity. I've always been a bit of a romantic, and tend to root for true love."

"Fine. Wouldn't want you getting all twitchy with that trigger finger. But I'm telling you now—it's *not* true love." She crossed her arms, annoyed, knowing there was nothing she could do but go hunting for the Hope.

"If ye say so, lassie."

She tried to think of a way to find help. Should she tell MacTavish of the tunnel and lead them to the necklace or try to delay them in the hope someone would come to their aid? Angus would be turning up before long, and if she could get back to Iain, then together, they might stand a fighting chance.

"There is something we recently noticed and I think it could lead to the necklace, but we've yet to check it out fully, and frankly, Iain's the one that knows the area. All the trees and caves look the same to me, and I don't have a clue where to find any of the landmarks being referenced.

And keep in mind that these are just stabs in the dark. We could still be way off base."

He looked at her for a long moment as if mulling things over and then called out. "Bring me Iain MacCraigh."

A moment later, Iain was shoved into the room. He immediately crossed to her side. "Are ye all right?"

Cat nodded, but MacTavish was having none of it. "Neither of ye will be doing well if we don't find the necklace, so I suggest we start moving before I lose patience. And let me make myself clear—if either of ye try something daft, it'll be the other one who'll pay the consequences."

As dangerous as these guys seemed, she had to try to send out a call for help. They might not get the chance once they were out in the woods. "Just one thing—we're both barefoot, since you caught us as we were getting up. If you want us to make it through those woods anytime this century, then I suggest letting us get our shoes, and frankly, I wouldn't mind a bit more clothing, since I'm still in my pj's."

"Only if ye make it quick." MacTavish glared at her as he waved his gun in the direction of the door. "Come on, then."

She headed for the door with Iain trailing at her side, their eyes locked on each other. She knew he might try to get help, but she doubted MacTavish would leave Iain alone, whereas she might be able to ask for some privacy. Her cell phone was upstairs, in addition to one of the home phones. If she could get away long enough to put a call in to the police, they might get out of the ordeal unscathed.

"You first." MacTavish stood at the door to her room and motioned her in. "The door stays open. Try anything, and I shoot the lad."

"Do I not get any privacy?"

"If ye want privacy, then I suggest ye stay in night-clothes. Now either get changed or let's get moving."

Frustrated, Cat grabbed clothes and, using the blanket off her bed for privacy, got dressed, knowing there'd be no chance of her making a call with him standing right there. She did, however, pick the jeans she was wearing the night before, knowing her cell phone was still tucked away in the pocket, and chose a sweater long enough to mask the bulge. If he didn't search her, then maybe she could find a moment to make a call. Iain was next to get dressed, and before long, they were out the door and heading for the trails. MacTavish had come prepared not only with a gun, but with rope and a pack of supplies and equipment.

The morning air was bitterly cold and a heavy mist fell upon them, shrouding them like a wet blanket, sucking every bit of her warmth and energy. Her jacket worked to keep her mostly dry, but there was little getting around the wet that clung to her skin and clothes, the damp wheedling its way to her very core.

Iain kept shooting her glances, his gaze intense as if trying to reassure her that things would work out. MacTavish trailed behind them, his gun never wavering, even as they started the climb up the hill with Iain leading the way.

They were heading to the tunnels, the mist changing to a bone-chilling rain. Cat wondered if Iain might lead them elsewhere to try and save the Hope from falling into MacTavish's hands, but evidently not. She supposed it was necessary, and in the end the necklace might not be there at all. In their predicament, she didn't know whether to hope for it to be found or for it to remain tucked away safe.

Cat's mind kept racing, jumping from one thought to another. She was desperate to find a way to get rid of MacTavish so they'd be safe, but her mind also kept straying to Iain and the words he'd spoken the night before. How could he possibly ask her to marry him? He couldn't be serious. Iain MacCraigh—married? The tabloids would have a field day—Scotland's most eligible bachelor proposing marriage after mere weeks. The gossip alone would have Iain backtracking faster than a politician on a campaign-time promise.

It'd be insane to marry him. And yet...

When exactly she'd fallen in love with him, she couldn't say, despite her best efforts to keep things casual between them. With a glance in

Iain's direction, she took him in—the dark stubble across his strong jaw, his dark disheveled locks wet with rain, and those piercing blue eyes that made her pulse flutter. And now, with a gun at their back, she might not ever get to tell him that she loved him. He might never know how she truly felt about him.

The climb grew steep, and despite her missteps, MacTavish and Iain managed the climb with little difficulty. When Iain tried to give her a hand, MacTavish growled at him to keep his distance.

Iain stopped where he was, holding onto a branch for support. "If ye're not going to let me help her, then at least let her go ahead of us, so I can help her if she falls."

"I'll manage, Iain." They both ignored her.

"How much farther?"

"Just ahead, but it's a steep climb from here to the cave's entrance." With jaw tight, Iain stood his ground, his eyes locked on MacTavish—but first he'd given her a quick glance.

It made her wonder if he was up to something. And if he was going to try something, when would he attempt it? The climb was indeed steep. Would it be a push down the hill with the hope of escape? Or wait until the darkness of the tunnels masked their movements.

"Very well—let her take the lead. But try anything and I'll put a bullet through ye. Are we clear?"

"Aye. We are." Iain turned away from MacTavish and gave her a small nod to tell her to continue on her way. "Be careful, love. It'll get steeper just before the entrance."

With the rain refusing to let up, Cat worked her way up the muddy slope, more often than not on all fours, grasping at whatever she could for a secure hold. She was nearly there. Pushing past the branches that partially obscured the opening from view, she pulled herself in. It seemed like too good an opportunity to pass up, when Iain would make it into the dark tunnel before MacTavish. She looked around for a branch to use as weapon, but there was little to be found.

Iain scrambled in and rushed to her side. "Get as far back as ye can. Go!"

"But—"

"Don't argue with me. Go, Cat. *Now.*"

She did as he asked, her pulse thundering as the adrenaline and fear kicked in. Yet why was it she suddenly wanted to tell him everything she'd kept bottled up inside? Why was it she desperately wanted to tell him that she loved him?

MacTavish started to climb into the tunnel when Iain tackled him, grabbing for the gun as a shot ricocheted off the rock wall, deafening in the small space. Cat held her breath as they struggled, each lurch driving them closer to the edge. Iain pounded MacTavish's hand against the rock face, knocking the gun away. Getting free of MacTavish's hold, Iain pushed him towards the edge, but the old man was still quick and strong, and before he went over the steep drop, he grabbed Iain.

And they were gone.

Panic sucked the breath from her lungs as she rushed over, hoping there was something there to break Iain's fall. A cry escaped her lips, not wanting to believe what she saw. He looked broken and mangled, his leg impaled on a broken branch. Slipping her way down the hill while grabbing at branches to slow her descent, she scooted towards them as fast as she could, hoping Iain was still alive. MacTavish seemed to have broken some of Iain's fall, catching the brunt of the injuries from the rocks below.

"*Iain.* Talk to me." She touched his cheek, hoping he'd come to. She glanced at his leg, wondering if she should remove the branch sticking through his leg, but worried she might cause the bleeding to increase. "Iain, please."

He was breathing. That was something, but she wasn't sure of what internal injuries he may have sustained. She tried her cell phone, but there was no reception.

"Cat…"

Relief flooded over her. "Bloody hell, Iain. You shouldn't have done it. Damn the necklace. You could have been killed."

"MacTavish?" His face tightened with pain as he tried to turn towards the reason they were in this mess.

She shifted over and checked the man's pulse, before taking a closer look. "I think he's dead. I'm afraid his head hit a rock. Your leg…"

"Best if we leave it. Call Angus. I don't want him stumbling onto the group at the house." He coughed and wheezed, making her heart lurch with worry.

"I have no reception. Maybe if I head back towards the house." The thought of leaving him in the condition he was in had her stomach knots.

"Call him and then call the police." He reached up to touch her face. "Don't look so worried, love. I'll manage."

"Damn it, Iain. I love you."

"Aye, lass. I know—and I love ye also. With all my heart." He coughed, the sound of it wet and rattling in his lungs. "Go, love. I'll manage 'til ye get back. And once ye do, I hope ye know I'll be marrying ye."

She blinked back her tears and kissed him. "I wouldn't have it any other way."

Cat watched as Iain was taken away on a stretcher and loaded into the ambulance. She had desperately wanted to go with him, but there was no room in the vehicle and the police still needed to speak to her. They'd already arrested the men who'd come with MacTavish, but there was still James and Malcolm to deal with. Malcolm might get off easy, depending on his involvement. But James? Well, he'd messed with the wrong girl for the last time.

Once inside, Cat answered their questions as best she could, itching to get to Iain's side. The cop she was dealing with was the same one who'd taken a statement from them after MacTavish first showed up, so he already knew of their previous troubles.

"I'll call when I have more information. I'm afraid I'll need you to stay in town until this is sorted." He got to his feet and flipped closed his notebook.

"There's one more thing." She went into the library, grabbed her laptop, and handed it to the police. "I'm sure you'll find the evidence you need. James may not have had anything to do with the men that were here, but he did hack into my computer with the purpose of stealing my research."

James, dealing with another officer, overheard her. "You wouldn't dare press charges." He went red in the face, stammering in his fury—as if Cat cared a flying whoop.

"Wouldn't I?"

The cop who'd taken her laptop turned a steely gaze on James. "I think it best you come with us to the station. I'm going to have some more questions for you."

With everyone else gone, Cat turned to Angus, her defenses finally crumbling as she fought back tears, overwhelmed with worry about Iain. "I don't know where the hospital is."

Angus put an arm around her shoulder and gave her a quick hug. "I'll take ye to him."

"You saw him—will he be ok?"

"I think so, lass."

CHAPTER
Twenty

H AVING DUG THROUGH the dirt wall blocking the metal gate from view, Iain and Angus now worked on cutting through the bolt. It had taken Iain several weeks to heal, and during that time Cat had refused to go back to the tunnel without him. With his leg finally allowing him to climb, they'd returned to see if they'd finally found the Highlander's Hope.

The bolt gave way, the metal weakened with age. Iain gave her a smile and then pulled the gate open, the hinges screeching in protest, the metal flaking off in sheets of rust. "After you, my love."

Cat held up her flashlight and stepped past him, pausing just long enough to kiss him before moving into the small chamber filled with wooden boxes. Perhaps they held weapons for Prince Charlie's return, documents or funds, but it was all overlooked when their beams of light rested on a nook carved into the dirt and the small wooden box nestled there.

"Iain… I think this is it." She looked over at him as he stepped to her side, placing a hand on her shoulder.

"Aye, love. And the honor should be yers."

"Here's a bit more light." Angus moved closer, holding up the bright lantern so she could set hers down.

It was a simple box, but Iain's family crest was carved into the lid, and it set his pulse racing at breakneck speed. Cat undid the latch and opened the lid, before peeling back the delicate fabric.

It sparkled in the torchlight like a million stars—the Highlander's Hope. Diamonds and emeralds, with smaller rubies and sapphires, were all worked into an exquisite piece of art.

She turned towards him, her smile beaming from ear to ear. "It's beautiful, Iain. Can you believe we've found it?"

"Aye, love. I had no doubt."

Back in the library with a roaring fire to get them warm, Iain watched as Cat documented everything into her laptop, and then proceeded to take notes and pictures of the Hope. He loved watching her work—the intensity of her gaze, her unwavering concentration, her contagious enthusiasm. His father had come in for a look, not quite believing they'd found it on MacCraigh land. Iain couldn't believe it either. But there was more on Iain's mind than the excitement about the necklace.

The last few weeks had been busy with doctor's appointments and visits to the police station, and they had not spoken about getting married since that fateful day with MacTavish. He'd been waiting for this moment—for her to find the Highlander's Hope. And now the time had come.

By the gods, he loved her with all his heart. When she got up to stretch her legs, he joined her and took her hand. "Come, love. Ye've been at it for hours. Some fresh air will do ye good."

Iain led her out towards the gardens, the day warm for December. There was a spot he'd always loved—looking out towards the craggy cliffs, and beyond that in the far distance, the sea. Standing behind her, he wrapped his arms around her and pulled her close.

"It's just gorgeous here, Iain." Cat leaned back against him, snuggling closer.

"I meant what I said, my love." Iain reached into his pocket and pulled out his mother's engagement ring. "I love ye, Cat. Will ye marry me?"

She spun in his arms to face him, her eyes locked on his. "Yes—I love you with all my heart, Iain. Of course I'll marry you."

He kissed her, long and sweet, his heart one with hers, his soul complete. When he could finally pull himself away, he slipped the diamond ring on her finger. "It was my mother's. She'd want ye to have it."

"Oh, Iain. It's beautiful." She threw her arms around his neck, kissing him once more.

"There's more, love. I heard from my accountant." It had taken some finagling but they somehow managed it. "I was able to free up enough cash to recoup the money my father fronted for my brother and to bail Malcolm out of his troubles."

"Iain… I hope you know that I understand why you'd use the necklace for collateral. I'd likely have done the same."

"No, love. Ye wouldn't have. But that's all right. It's one of the reasons I love ye."

"You know, the tabloids are going to have a field day with this."

"Aye, love. I expect they will." He couldn't help but laugh at the thought of the headlines they'd dream up.

Cat smiled and gave him a quick kiss. "Except that none of this ever happened."

He burst out laughing and swept her off her feet in a spin until she squealed in delight. "Of course not, my love. It's already forgotten."

THE END

Made in the USA
Lexington, KY
26 November 2013